VENT REVISITED

THE SECOND FILL IN THE BLANK ADULT READER PARTICIPATION BOOK THAT IS GUARANTEED TO MAKE YOU LAUGH, THINK, AND VENT YOUR FRUSTRATIONS. IT MIGHT EVEN CHANGE A FEW OF YOUR OPINIOINS.

OTHER PUBLISHED NOVELS BY ROBERT K. SWISHER JR.
Historical Fiction: Trade and E-book
Published by Sunstone Press
The Land
Fatal Destiny

Contemporary Western Fiction: Trade and E-book
PUBLISHED BY SUNSTONE PRESS
How Far the Mountain
The Last Narrow Gauge Train Robbery
The Last Day in Paradise
Love Lies Bleeding
The Man From the Mountain

Literary: Out of Print
Published by Samisdat Press - Canada
American Love Story

Young Adult: Trade Only
Published by Echo Press California
The Weaver
Published by Sunstone Press
Only Magic
Humor: E-book only
Conversations With the Golf God
Mystery Series: E-book only:
Bob Roosevelt Mystery Series – 4 novels

Contemporary Fiction: E-book only
Hope
How Bridge McCoy Learned to Say I Love you
A Circle Around Forever
Satire: Trade and E-book
Published by Open Talon Press
Vent
Grammar Nazis Are Not Always Rite, Right, Write
Vent Revisited

Short stories and poetry in literary journals, articles in outdoor magazines.
Reviews by Publishers Weekly, Best Sellers, Library Journal, and many others.

VENT REVISITED

by

Robert K. Swisher Jr.

Robert K. Swisher Jr.

PUBLISHED BY
OPEN TALON PRESS

EDITORS: Liz Gaidry and Brad C. Walker
COVER DESIGNER: Sharon Brownlie

Library of Congress - In Publication Date
Swisher, Robert K, 1947 -
Vent Revisited: A novel / by Robert K. Swisher Jr.
Summary: A humorous and satirical reader participation book covering both absurd and pertinent topics.
ISBN: 978-0-9978096-2-3
LCN: 2018935640

TABLE OF CONTENTS

DEDICATION

FOR THOSE WHO PONDER WHAT EXACTLY IS ALTERNATIVE TRUTH?

CHAPTER ONE

A LETTER TO THE READER

Dear Reader:

For those of you who purchased the first Vent book, thank you for purchasing the second. For those of you new to the Vent books you are in for a different reading experience. Vent and Vent Revisited are unique and groundbreaking as they are adult interactive books. Besides being the story of two slightly off center people accidentally meeting and becoming great friends, you will be asked questions that run the gamut from modern world problems, politics, and the utterly ridiculous things many people take seriously. Do not fret. This is not a test. If you purchased a print copy all you have to do for each question you simply circle YES or NO and write your comments on the provided lines. If you purchased an e-book you can state your answers and comments either verbally or mentally. Unlike the print copy the e-book does not have lines but blank spaces. There is no content lost with the e-book compared to the print copy. In fact, many of us who rarely write longhand might find it easier. About the only thing I write longhand anymore is my name on a credit card receipt.

Here is an example of a question:

Are alternative facts, in truth, nothing but lies? Circle YES...NO...and then there will be either a series of lines to write your opinion or a space for you to take the time to state your opinion.

Because this is a reader participation book let me emphatically state you do not have to write your name, social security number, bank account password, or any personal information in this book. If you have a book that asks for any personal information, gives a P.O. box in either Nigeria, Florida, or New Jersey to mail the book to when you are finished, BEWARE, it is a scam – telephone the police immediately and report the issue even though they will not be able to do anything about it anyway – in fact they might be taking a piece of the action.

There are four purposes for this novel. One is to give you an opportunity to vent your frustrations over the happenings in our modern world. Two is to give you the opportunity to laugh without the fear of being embarrassed. Three, you will be able to state or write your personal opinion without being cut off half way through your comment by some obnoxious, loudmouthed idiot, who doesn't agree with you. And four, there are scattered pieces of information the mainstream news and various state and federal government agencies do not want you to know that I feel every person should be aware of.

I highly recommend Vent and Vent Revisited for reading groups. Each question can be easily debated and it will also give you the courage to state ideas you have kept hidden because you are worried people might think you are stupid. There is no need to worry, we are all stupid at one time or another – normally more times than not. For example – look at the people we elect to be our leaders. To be fair I include members of all political parties and persuasions. But, the question is, who elects these idiots?

Out of the goodness of my heart I will warn you that there are some questions in this book that might offend you. Please, if you do get offended, do not say any derogatory remarks about my mother, she is old and had nothing to do with this book. You may e-mail me and call me anything you want. After spending time in a war, been a hippie, a cowboy, married, divorced, and raised three children, I have been called about everything one can be called.

Vent is not intended for children – although in our modern world the bad language that at times I use in the book is in most children's vocabulary by the time they are six. If you let your children go to PG movies, look at the magazine covers by the checkout at the grocery store, watch pro and college football cheerleaders, watch the Oscars, go to the beach or swimming pool, or partake of the nightly news, no child will be introduced to any information that, when they are older, they can use as an excuse why they are hooked on Tootsie Rolls or it is your fault their lives are ruined.

Now get ready to laugh, think, and vent.

Sincerely,

Robert K. Swisher Jr.

CHAPTER TWO

THE STORY CONTINUES

For those of you who did not read the first Vent I am William Brown, 66 years old and presently living in Phoenix, Arizona. My wife divorced me ten years ago for a younger man who drove a silver Jaguar. I have no children and only recently started a relationship with a wonderful lady named Julia who is also divorced. Her husband left her for a 19 year old pole dancer who wants to be a doctor. Julia and I enjoy each other's company immensely but neither of us has ever mentioned love – either we are afraid or at our age it is not really that important. She is a retired nurse and now donates her time helping people that are homebound. Her grown children live out of state which in many ways pleases both of us. She, like I, have completely downsized our lives, selling our houses, and moving into small apartments. I make a better than average living selling cars although I feel no great pride in my job. Selling something that is polluting the air we breathe, even though cars in our modern world are a necessary evil, is not exactly something one should be proud of. But, like most things in modern life, paying the bills takes precedence over many morally wrong endeavors. If you do not believe internal combustible engines pollute you should stop reading this book, drive your car into the garage, shut the garage door, keep the engine running, and repeat over and over again as many times as you can before you pass out and die, "There is no such thing as pollution, there is no such thing as pollution."

Or, you can stay alive and answer this question? Is the mixture of grey, green, and brown colors smothering the majority of the large cities of the world the true color of the sky? Circle YES or NO...

If you answered YES have you ever seen blue sky or is blue sky an alternative truth? Circle either YES or NO...

Here is a space for you explain where all that green, gray, and brown air goes?

____

____

Where does that multi colored air come from?

____

Do you believe that coal smoke, wood smoke, car emissions, truck emissions, diesel fuel, pesticides, chemical fertilizers, and many other man made substances in anyway have impacted the environment? Circle either YES or NO...

If your answer is NO here is a space to explain your reasoning:

____

____

Do you believe that mankind has in anyway contributed to climate change? Circle YES or NO…

If you circled NO do you believe that 99 and 9/10's of all the scientist in the world who believe in climate change are lying? Circle YES or NO...

If they are lying do you think that they are planning on becoming politicians or maybe even running for president? Circle YES or NO...

Also, if you believe they are lying why would they? A space for your reasoning:

____

____

Merely out of curiosity would you quench your thirst from a river that runs through any of our metropolitan cities? Circle YES or NO...

If you answered No why not? Your answer:

____

Earlier last year, after attending a relative's funeral in Iowa and due to poor visibility during a severe rain storm, I missed my return flight to Phoenix from Kansas City and got lost downtown. Waiting in my rental car the rain turned into a slight drizzle and a man hurried by who was waving his arms up and down and holding a heated conversation with himself. He was slightly older than I am, so skinny he made a scarecrow look fat. He had salt and pepper mid-length hair and was clean shaven. He had bushy dark brown eyebrows and his eyes were large and so blue they pierced the drab day like blue silver dollars. The throng of umbrella carrying people parted before him like he was either Moses or had a deathly contagious disease. For some unexplainable reason I was intrigued by the man and with no regard for the light rain I followed him to a bar where I introduced myself to Samuel L. Ruthorford Jr. After an afternoon and early evening of drinking beer, eating a hamburger, having two cups of coffee that were so strong I did not sleep for two days, and a final cocktail I came to realize why Samuel L. Ruthorford Jr. was nick-named Vent. The mention of any controversial topic would make Vent twitch and lurch about like he had fleas and go into a loud dissertation a Baptist preacher would be proud of. A few of the topics we discussed were the police, gay marriage, taxes, drugs, homelessness, immigration, gun control, race, the forfeiture laws, women in combat, the randomness of fate, and why a restroom is really not a restroom. I also discovered, during our far too short time together, I possessed a deep affinity for Vent. He was the brother I never had, a confidant, an inspiration, and he made me look at the world in a way that the absurdity no longer affected me in a negative way. During our short time together I learned he had written half-a-dozen novels but never submitted them to agents or publishers – they rested in boxes in a closet gathering dust and bemoaning their fate. He served in Vietnam like I did, tried a brief stint at being a hippie, attended college before joining the ranks of the mainstream world, and with a small amount of money he saved in the army bought a new stock called Apple which made him a small fortune. Even though rich he does not own a fancy watch or wear jewelry and lives in a modest apartment in downtown Kansas City. I also learned he had been deeply in love but his wife had died. When they decided to have children it was too late.

When I said goodbye to Vent he gave me a card with his address on it explaining he did not have a phone of any kind, a computer, I pad, or a lap top, and he never wrote letters. It made me sad thinking I would never see him again. Also, it made me want to ask him why he had a business card if he possessed no modern forms of communication. But, I decided it was not a good question.

Several months later feeling nostalgic I wrote Vent a letter even though I felt he would not reply. A few weeks later, much to my surprise and happiness, I received a short letter informing me he would be visiting Phoenix in December and we could vent over many of the new topics that have people all over the country in a state of exasperation or downright disbelief. He said there was no need to reply, gave me his flight number and the arrival time with instructions I should pick him up outside the baggage claim. He did not state he was staying at a hotel, with a friend, or if he wanted to stay with me. I applied for and set up several vacation days from work for the time Vent would be in town.

It was December 16 at 4 p.m. and 76 degrees when Vent emerged out of the airport. Unlike the first time I saw him, when he was wearing a rumpled out dated suit, he was now dressed in khaki cargo pants, a blue cotton shirt, with an off gray sport jacket, brown socks, and brown leather shoes polished to a high sheen. There was a canvas tote bag hanging from his shoulder and he was pulling a small suitcase with a heavy winter coat strapped to it. His hair was cut neatly and in place and his eyebrows were trimmed. He reminded me of an English professor from an expensive liberal arts college. I thought it slightly out of character that Vent was not tossing his arms up and down and twitching like he had fleas while talking to himself but was walking as calmly as one can outside of a busy airport. I waved. Vent hurried to the car. The first words he said to me were not, "Hello, good to see you William, I'm glad you are on time," but in a level not greatly excited voice asked, "William, do you think we live in a free country?" which I will ask you: Is America a free country? Circle YES or NO...and several lines for your comment:

____

____

I answered "yes," expecting Vent to go into a loud tirade with a great deal of arm gyrations. Instead, Vent merely rolled his large blue eyes back in their sockets and said in only a slightly agitated voice, "You mean to tell me that working eight to twelve hours a day so you can afford to eat and have a place to live is being free?"

I started to reply but he went on. "You mean to tell me that being allowed two or three weeks vacation a year is being free," he said.

I tried to reply again to no avail. "You mean to tell me that paying taxes on everything you earn or buy is being free," he said.

"Maybe mankind has to change the definition of freedom," I said.

Out of curiosity what countries do you think enjoy more freedom than the United States: I will start - Sweden and Denmark:

Do you think Russian citizens have as much freedom as we do? Circle YES or NO...and a space for your reasoning:

"Even if you think you are free it is good to see you," Vent said. "I have missed our conversations. There are only a few people I enjoy talking to in Kansas City."

"It is good to see you also," I replied sincerely.

"Anyplace in particular you would like to go? I asked Vent.

"There has to be a happy hour somewhere close by," he said, adding, "I understand now why people come to Arizona in the winter. The temperature is delightful. When I left Kansas City it was 27 degrees and snowing.

"If you had your choice would you spend the winter shoveling snow or putting on suntan lotion? Circle your answer: SNOW...SUNTAN LOTION.

If you circled SNOW I would seriously consider enrolling in some form of therapy or start sniffing cocaine and become a skier.

Question? Is cocaine the choice of drugs for the ski crowd? Circle YES or NO…

The answer is YES. In fact at the majority of ski resorts a gram of cocaine is cheaper than a lift ticket.

Merely for information sake there is more cocaine being imported into the country now than ever before.

The establishment we headed to is unique in more ways than one. One afternoon after picking up my laundry at a strip mall I noticed several well dressed people going in a door located on the side of the building. I thought it odd as there was no sign over the door nor were there any windows. For some reason, besides common sense, I was drawn to the door. Once inside I was surprised to discover I was in an expensively furnished bar. There were several dozen tables with red leather chairs scattered around a large circular bar and there was a small stage and dance floor in the back. An enormous flat screen T.V. was showing horse races. Eight middle-aged, well dressed men, wearing enough gold chains and gold watches to put a dent in Fort Knox were sitting on the far side of the bar facing the door. Two men were playing cards at a corner table – also facing the door. Everyone's conversation stopped in mid-sentence when they saw me and I knew I should have minded my own business, but, being at least half of a manly man I did not turn around. The bartender, a big strapping fellow, who looked like his hobby was ripping people's noses off, asked me in a gruff Italian accent, "Hey, you know where you are?"

Feeling no need to lie I replied, "No."

"Who do you work for?" he asked.

"I sell cars," I replied.

For some reason all the patrons started laughing hysterically like the word no and the phrase selling cars possessed a humorous side to them that I had never known. One of the men waved me to come over saying in an authoritative tone, "Come on in and have a drink on me."

As I started to sit a man about the size of a houseboat came towards me holding out his hand in a way I knew I was supposed to wait. He proceeded to expertly frisk me. Satisfied I was not carrying a knife, gun, grenade, or bazooka he nodded at the man who had waved me over. "Nothing personal," the frisker said in a tone I knew if he had found a weapon I might be missing my legs or at least one arm. "You could get a job for the TSA," I told him.

"They don't pay enough," he replied.

Over the next several hours I came to the conclusion, without asking or being told, I was in a private mob bar. There was Fat Tony, Slim Jim, Johnny the Wart, Billie Bundle, Frank the Nose, and others with obscure names. After several drinks, which I never paid for, I was informed I could come whenever I wanted but could only bring one guest at a time. Women were only allowed on Saturday night, which was dance night. There was no food but it could be ordered in. For their generosity I understood it would be nice if I would give discounts on cars to all the members of the club, their friends, wives, mistresses, distant cousins, parents, and children over 16. Over the past several months I have sold a lot of cars making about $100 a car – a good deal when mixed drinks at the bar are only $4.00 and beers are $2.00. Most bars in Phoenix drinks are at least $10.00 and beer is five to six dollars. One thing about the bar I enjoy is there is never any conversation about work – at least when I am around.

As we drove I told Vent about the bar. "Capitalism is the most organized crime and politicians are the bosses," he said with little emotion and no twitching and squirming.

"I didn't use to think that way but I do now," I replied.

Do you think governments and organized crime have a lot in common? Circle YES or NO...and a space to list what they have in common:

____

____

"If you had a choice would you trust the President or a major crime boss?" Vent asked not raising his voice or even twitching a little bit. Circle your answer: PRESIDENT...CRIME BOSS...and a space for you to explain your reasoning:

____

____

Much to my surprise the bar was empty. The bartender nodded as Vent and I sat at the bar. "They only have Italian beer," I said.

"Do you have Moretti?" Vent asked.

"Does most Italian food have tomatoes in it?" the bartender answered in a way I did not know if he was trying to be funny or sarcastic.

Vent did not bother to answer.

We both ordered a Moretti. Italian beers do not excite me much, but on the other hand Italian food has never been my favorite. I am not a big fan of cooked tomatoes or garlic.

Truthfully, do you like cooked tomatoes or garlic? Circle YES or NO...

If you like garlic do you believe in vampires? Circle YES or NO...

"You sell cars like William?" the bartender asked Vent as he placed the beers with cold glasses in front of us.

"No, I mind my own business," Vent said.

"I like you, you a smart guy. Most people today want to stick their noses in every one's business," the bartender chuckled and moved to the far side of the bar.

Do you think the world would be a better place if the majority of people minded their own business? Circle YES or NO...

Why can't most people mind their own business?

____

____

Vent and I clinked our glasses together. "To the randomness of life," I said.

"And stupidity," Vent added.

After a few swallows and a short period of silence I said. "Vent, you don't seem as excitable and high strung as the first time we met."

"The way the country is divided and being run by self centered idiots I have decided all the jerking around and arm tossing was a waste of energy," Vent replied. "I now vent in a dignified manner. I do not want people to think I have been overcome by the stupidity of our leaders."

Question? Do you think America is being run by idiots and that most of the people the President has surrounded himself with really don't care about the American people? Circle YES or NO...

Do you think the government cares more for rich people than the middle class? Circle YES or NO...and a space for your reasoning:

____

____

Do you think the government cares more for the middle class than the poor? Circle YES or NO...your reasoning:

____

____

Do you think the government really cares about the poor? Circle YES or NO...

If they do care about the poor why are there slums? A space for your answer:

____

____

Do you think the United States is more divided now than it ever has been? Circle your answer YES or NO...your reasoning:

____

____

Do you think the world is more divided now than it ever has been? Circle your answer YES or NO..,

Or has the world always been a mess and with instant news we now know how messed up the world really is? Circle your answer YES or NO...

Do you know that your fearless fake tanned leader just signed legislation that makes it harder for workers to draw overtime? Circle YES or NO...

The answer is YES. All you hard working people that voted for Trump enjoy less pay.

Should a company have to pay overtime? Circle YES or NO...a space for your reasoning:

____

____

"Now that you are calmer and more dignified do you think that without all the gyrations and twitching around expelling frustrations from your system, you will develop ulcers?" I asked Vent.

"Did you know the majority of ulcers are not caused from frustration or anxiety but from an imbalance of microbes in your stomach? Vent said sounding like the science guy on TV.

"I'll be," I said.

Question? Did you know that the majority of ulcers are caused by pesky little microbes that live in your stomach? Circle YES or NO...

Do you really care if your microbes are balanced? Circle YES or NO...

For those of you who do care run as fast as you can to the grocery store and buy fifty cartons of unsweetened yogurt. If you buy sweetened yogurt you will still balance your microbes but will put on about 35 unwanted pounds.

"Do you think people who are bigoted and filled with hate are this way because the microbes in their brains are not balanced?" I asked.

"No, they are just ignorant," Vent said with a hint of disdain, "but there is a study that says microbial activity in your stomach does have an effect on your brain."

Do you think bigoted and hate filled people are just ignorant or can you blame it on microbes? Circle YES...NO...MICROBES...

If they are not ignorant what are they?

____

____

"I find it highly confusing that the majority of all the worlds past wars and the modern wars, at their roots, are religions fighting religions," Vent said dropping the subject about ignorant people.

"I think the Muslim God does not like the Christian God, and the Christian God does not like the Jewish God, and the Muslim God does not like the other Muslim Gods, and the Baptist God does not like the Mormon God, and all the Hindu Gods do not like the Buddhist God, and the Russian Orthodox God does not like the Catholic God, and all combinations of religions do not like any other combination of religions," I said making myself mentally dizzy.

If most wars are fought over religion is religion then in all truth a bad thing? Circle your answer: YES or NO...and a space for your reasoning:

____

____

Is there only one God and man has invented all the others? Circle YES or NO...

But, if there are many, many Gods, which one is the true God?

A space for your answer:

____

If your God is the true God does He or She want you to kill people? Circle YES...NO...

Does He or She want you to feed the poor? Circle YES or NO...

Does He or She want you to help the homeless? Circle YES or NO...

Does He or She want you to assist immigrants? Circle YES or NO…

If your answers are YES why do so many people who profess to be religious kill people, could care less about the less fortunate, and want the government to build a wall along our border with Mexico? A space for your reasoning:

____

____

Since the beginning of mankind there has been a steady succession of gods and deities. Do you think these gods and deities have failed? Circle YES or NO...

If you think they have not failed what have the gods and deities accomplished? A space for you to list their accomplishments:

____

____

There has been a strong movement in the United States government, ever since President Johnson for all politicians to state reverently "AND GOD BLESS AMERICA." Before Johnson politicians did not count on God for votes. In the United States there are Catholics, Jews, Baptists, Lutherans, Episcopalians, Evangelicals, Jehovah Witnesses, Mormons, Quakers, Methodists, Mennonites, Amish, Born Agains, Snake Worshipers, Muslims, and a multitude of other religions. Each of these religions deems their God to be something different from the other religion's God. So in truth should our political leaders be saying "AND ALL OF THE MULTITUDES OF GODS BLESS AMERICA" or should they tell the truth and say, "AND THE GOD OF MONEY AND GREED BLESS AMERICA?" Circle YES or NO...and a space for you to list how many different gods you think there are in America:

____

____

Vent and I finished our beers and ordered another one.

"What do you think about our new President?" I asked.

“No matter what I think about him he won the Electoral College by having the majority votes of the Super Delegates,” Vent said dodging my question.

“But he lost the popular vote,” I said.

“Presidential and Vice Presidential candidates don’t care about the popular vote. They say the phrase, ‘for the American People’ merely to convince you they really care about the common man.”

“You mean in all truth our vote means nothing?” I said.

“Partially true,” Vent replied. “A Super Delegate for the Democratic Party does not have to cast his or her vote for whoever received the majority of votes in their state.

But the Super Delegates for the Republican Party have to follow the voting of their state.”

After this years election everyone should know what a Super Delegate is. What is a Super Delegate? I will give you a clue. A Super Delegate has nothing to do with the Super Bowl:

For those of you who do not know what a Super Delegate is take a few minutes and Google Super Delegate. That is unless you have a desire to stay uninformed.

Now that you know what a Super Delegate is do you think your vote really means anything for President and Vice President? Circle YES or NO...and a space for your reasoning:

If you believe in a Super Delegate do you think the position of Super Delegate should be filled by a popular vote and not by appointment? Circle YES or NO...

Who created Super Delegates? Circle REPUBLICAN PARTY or DEMOCRATIC PARTY:

The answer is the Democratic Party.

Do you believe that the Electoral College should be removed and only the popular vote used to elect the President and Vice President? Circle YES or NO... and a space for your reasoning:

____

____

The founding fathers stipulated an Electoral College because they feared a direct vote by the people for President and Vice President could lead to the election of a tyrant.

Do you think without and Electoral College a tyrant could rise to power in the United States? Circle YES or NO...your reasoning:

____

____

"Besides the fact Trump won the Electoral College and therefore is our president what do you think of him?" I asked again.

"It isn't so much what I think of him that worries me but what worries me are the members of his party that feel obligated to follow and defend a person of his character," Vent said. "He is a liar and denigrates handicapped people and women. He made his fortune by not paying people who worked for him and declaring bankruptcy so many times American banks stopped loaning him money. All of which is public knowledge and yet people follow him. I don't understand. All it proves is there are many people, including politicians, who have no common sense or decency."

Do you think it is true that many people have little common sense or decency? Circle YES or NO…

If you had a daughter and she wanted to date a man with the background of Trump would you let her? Circle YES or NO...

If you had a gay son and Trump was gay would you want your son bringing Trump home for dinner? Circle YES or NO...

If Trump was transgender would you let him use your bathroom? Circle YES or NO...

Do you think the characteristics of Trump's speeches and attitudes has led to the rise in hate crimes in the United States? Circle YES or NO...and a space for your reasoning:

____

____

Do you think that Trump has drained the swamp or added more mud back into the swamp? Circle DRAINED or ADDED MORE MUD.

Do you think that because of Trump many people around the world dislike Americans more than they used to? Circle YES or NO...

If you were a Canadian would you like Americans? Circle YES or NO...

If you were a Mexican would you like Americans? Circle YES or NO...

Do you think that America is so big and strong that we do not need allies?

Circle YES or NO...your reasoning:

____

____

If Trump decided to invade China would you volunteer to go to the front? Circle YES or NO…

How about invading Russia? Circle YES or NO...

How about North Korea? Circle YES or NO...

"Why is it that most people who were never in the military always seem to be the ones that want to go to war?" Vent asked. A space for your answer:

____

____

More than 50% of Americans are tired of the war in Afghanistan. Politicians are always proclaiming how our soldiers in Afghanistan are protecting our freedom. How does the war in Afghanistan or Syria have anything to do with our freedom? A space for your answer:

____

Trump for years stated if he was put in power he would immediately withdraw all troops from Afghanistan. He is now sending more troops. If your child lied as often as Trump does what would you do to your child? A space for your answer:

Out of curiosity, do you think that China would let the United States invade North Korea? Circle your answer YES or NO...

Did you know that when America backed out of the Trans Pacific Partnership China stepped in immediately and took the United States place as the chief trader and power broker? Circle your answer YES or NO...

Do you know that the main looser with the United States backing out of the Trans Atlantic Partnership is the American farmer? Circle YES or NO...and that countries are already making deals with each other while excluding the United States.

Did you know that Mexico is the largest importer of American corn? YES or NO... and that from day one when Trump started talking about building a wall along the Mexican border Mexico and China have been expanding their trade. Mexico has also expanded trade with South America.

"I really don't want to talk about Trump," Vent said. "I would rather be the proverbial Ostrich with his head stuck in the sand and everything will go away."

If you ignore what is going on in the world will it all go away? YES or NO...

But would you be happier? Circle YES or NO...

And, if you did not keep up with the news of the world would it really make any difference? Circle YES or NO...

To follow Vent's wishes I asked, "Vent, do you follow any sports if for no other reason than to forget about the real world?"

"At one time in my life I thought people who followed sports more than they followed the news were about as smart as a frog but now I feel even frogs have a descent amount of intelligence." Vent said.

"What made you change your mind?" I asked.

"Life and politics and the dismal state of the world can become so depressing and complicated there has to be some form of outlet or the majority of mankind would go crazy," Vent said resolutely.

Do you think even with sports the majority of mankind is crazy? Circle YES or NO...your reasoning:

____

____

Do you think even frogs have a small amount of intelligence? Circle YES or NO...

Do you think a frog would make a good politician? Circle YES or NO...and a space for your reasoning:

____

____

"Do you think the government would rather have you more interested in sports than in what they are doing?" I asked Vent.

"Of course, government's main purpose is to perpetuate itself and to succeed it must gain more and more power. The less people know what is going on the more power government can acquire," Vent said.

Do you think the above statement is true? Circle YES or NO...

Do you think it will ever change? Circle YES or NO...

Do you think more people are more interested in sports than what the government is doing? Circle YES or NO...

"There is a great amount of charity in the world that has nothing to do with politics," I said.

"True," Vent agreed, "but there is far more greed."

Do you think there is more greed in the world than charity?" Circle YES or NO...

If you circled NO why are there starving people all over the world?

____

____

If you circled YES is there anything that will help?

During a war each opposing army prays to God for protection and victory. Does this seem strange to you or only me? Circle your answer YES or NO...

Does each army have a different God? Circle YES or NO...

When one of the armies is defeated does their God join the winning armies God?

Circle YES or NO...

Or in all truth are both armies praying to the same God and really don't know it?

Circle YES or NO...

Can God be a trickster? Circle YES or NO...your reasoning:

Nothing to do with God but several presidents of the United States have become president by saying over and over again – MAKE AMERICA GREAT AGAIN. Has America ever been great? Circle YES or NO...

Seems to me the United States has been in and out of wars since the pilgrims landed on Plymouth Rock: numerous wars with the Native Americans, Revolutionary War, Whiskey War, War with Mexico, Civil War. We have been besieged with race issues (blacks vs. whites, Irish vs.

Germans, Chinese as indentured servants and on and on.) The United States has always had religious issues. Long before the present day Muslim phobia the Protestants were extremely good at killing Mormons and Catholics. Here is a blank for someone to please tell me when America was great?

____

____

For information sake the KKK's rallying point has always been the slogan "MAKE AMERICA GREAT AGAIN."

"If you don't have a place to stay you are welcome to stay with me. I have two bedrooms," I said, never being one who believes America was ever as great as it proudly states.

"Thank you for your generous offer but I have a hotel room. I don't think I will be here more than two or three days. Plus they have a free breakfast."

"Will you have more time for us to talk?" I asked wishing Vent would be staying longer and thinking he must think I don't eat breakfast or I am a lousy cook. The fact I am a lousy cook is beside the point.

"When I finish my appointment each day we can meet," he said in such a way I gathered he was not overly excited concerning his appointments.

I wanted to ask him what his appointments were but it was not my business. If he wanted to tell me he would. I did notice Vent seemed tired and slightly pasty in color although the majority of people from the Midwest look pasty during the winter. The Midwest is not known for it sunshine filled winter months, but more for an overcast gray sky that each passing day becomes more and more depressing and starts to seep into one's skin until by the end of winter people from the Midwest look like they have been in solitary confinement for ten or fifteen years, which does have one redeeming factor, it diminishes one's chances of getting skin cancer, although it has a person's cells screaming desperately for Vitamin D.

Vent signaled for another round of beers. Tired and pasty looking had not changed his ability to drink beer.

"What do you think about North Korea developing a nuclear capability?" Vent asked.

"I don't think much about it," I said. "If North Korea was ever stupid enough to fire a rocket at the United States their country would be reduced to a burning cinder quicker than their leader Kim Jong Un could say, 'Damn, I think I made a mistake.' In my opinion the United States is only stoking people's fears by keeping North Korea in the news."

Are you afraid of North Korea? Circle YES or NO... a space for your reasoning:

____

____

Are you afraid of an ant? Circle YES or NO...

Are you afraid of a child? Circle YES or NO...

If you were carrying a baseball bat would you be afraid of a guy with a pair of chop sticks? Circle YES or NO...

Canada has nuclear weapons. Are you afraid of Canada? Circle YES or NO...

You never know. Those sneaky Canadians might be scheming to overthrow our government, give everyone universal healthcare and a livable wage, and rig the NHL so they can win a Stanly Cup.

Back to being afraid - are you afraid of Saudi Arabia? Circle YES or NO...

Saudi Arabia is where Bin Laden was from. We keep them armed with all of our sophisticated weapons as well as arming other Middle East countries. Should we keep selling weapons to countries that in all truth do not like us? Circle YES or NO...

Did you know that Saudi Arabia has people who belong to Trump's golf courses that are lobbying to try and stop people from being able to sue Saudi Arabia for their roll in the destruction of the Twin Towers? Circle YES or NO...

The answer is YES.

If we are afraid of Muslim countries why do we sell them weapons? Your answer:

____

____

Do we sell them weapons because the United States is afraid Syria will attack the United States? Circle YES or NO...

If we are afraid Syria will attack us, how can they? A space for your answer:

____

Do you really and truly understand what is going on in the Middle East? Circle YES or NO...

Here is a quick run down. Saudi Arabia, which is Muslim, does not like the Muslims in Syria, nor the Muslims in Qatar – they are all different sects much like Lutherans and Baptists and Born Again Christians do not like each other but they are in common accord in the fact they do not like Jehovah's Witnesses. The Kurds which are on our side, which ever side that is, are fighting for independence from Turkey which is also on our side, but Turkey bombs the Kurds whenever they get a chance. The Turks and the Saudi's do not really like each other either. The United States trains groups from all sides and sells them weapons even though there are factions in every Middle Eastern country that supports ISIS. Groups that do not like us get weapons from us because at the moment they are fighting ISIS where a few years ago they were fighting us. Do you understand better now? Circle either YES or NO...Here are several lines for you to explain what you think is going on in the Middle East:

To add confusion to the Middle East the United States is fighting a war in Afghanistan to stop Al-Qaeda, who we backed when they were fighting the Russians, but who helps ISIS. Most Al-Qaeda fighters live and train in Pakistan, who is our ally, but really doesn't like us at all because we have better trade deals with India who is their sworn enemy (a small border issue). To top it off both Pakistan and India have nuclear weapons. And, guess who gave them nuclear weapons? I will give you a hint. It is a country that professes to be the biggest democracy in the world. A space for your answer:

____

____

Are you afraid of Pakistan and India now that you know they have nuclear weapons? Circle YES or NO...

Can any country where we presently have combat troops stationed attack the United States? Circle your answer YES or NO...

If your answer is NO who are we afraid of?

____

____

If your answer was YES what country or countries could attack us?

____

____

"If we have more nuclear weapons than any other country in the world why shouldn't all countries be able to have nuclear weapons?" Vent asked.

“I suppose we are afraid they will use them,” I replied.

“We are the only country to ever drop a nuclear weapon on people,” Vent said with a puzzled look.

If every country had weapons of mass destruction would the world be safer? Circle your answer YES or NO... and your reasoning:

____

____

Question? Do you enjoy watching the news and being in a constant state of fear or agitation? Circle YES or NO...

“Is more than half of what we are conditioned to be afraid of a real threat? Circle YES or NO...

The bartender brought the beers with two fresh chilled glasses. We toasted to fear.

“I have a question that has really been bothering me,” I said while my mind was still going around and around in circles trying to decipher the nuclear weapon and Middle East fiasco. “What is your opinion about the opiate pain killer epidemic that is sweeping the country?”

“Great marketing and use of the law,” Vent said.

“You have to be kidding,” I said.

Vent shook his head. “Oxycodone, the number one opiate pain killer in the world is manufactured by Purdue Pharma. Without getting into specific details, except the fact Oxycodone is a pain reliever that has been developed to slow release for up to twelve hours, there is close to 8 tons of the drug manufactured a year. The Sackler family who developed Oxycodone is one of the twenty richest families in America. Oxycodone is distributed all over the world. It is the most prescribed pain killer on the market. The only bad side effect being it is extremely habit forming. The drug cartels buy Oxycodone in huge quantities from pharmacies in South and Central America while the biggest suppliers of opiate pain killers in the United States are doctors and clinics."

"If the government knows the harm all opiate pain killers can cause why don't they do something about it?" I asked.

"Drug company's own politicians." Vent said. "If you don't believe me look at the laws governing the drug company's distribution of pain pills. It is not unusual for small pharmacies in remote parts of the country to get shipments of millions of tabs of pain killers and the DEA cannot touch them."

Is the above statement true or false?

It is true. The law protecting clinics went through the House and Senate without one negative vote.

"Don't doctors know better than to prescribe so many opiates?" I asked.

"Money has a way of changing people's attitudes," Vent said. "Even doctors."

With the harm that opiate based pain killers cause should they be taken off the market? Circle your answer YES or NO...

"How hard is it to get pain killers? I asked.

"About as hard as finding a gas station," Vent said.

If you wanted a pain killer right now and did not have a legitimate prescription from a doctor could you buy Oxycodone or the equivalent where you live? Circle YES or NO...

Would it be easier to get Oxycodone or heroin? Circle your answer OXYCODONE or

HEROIN.

Why do you think there are so many people taking drugs and completely destroying any sense of reality? Your answer:

____

____

Is reality all that bad? Circle YES or NO...

Do you think non-violent drug users should be put in jail or given help? Circle JAIL or HELP...

Can the United States control drugs? Circle your answer YES or NO...

If you answered YES how long has the war on drugs been going on? Circle your answer: 5 years...7 years...10...years...15 years...25 years... and your answer is ____.

The answer is 45 years. The official War on Drugs was launched in 1971 with the aid of Nancy Reagan.

Do you think since 1971 there has been a significant decrease in the use of drugs? Circle YES or NO...

Do you think there has been an increase in the different types of drugs that are available? Circle YES or NO...

I stated this earlier but do you know that heroin and cocaine production are at their highest levels ever recorded. Circle YES or NO...

The answer is YES. Why do you think this is true?

____

____

If Prohibition did not work why would the War on Drugs work? A blank for your answer:

____

____

What is the difference between the War on Drugs and Prohibition?

____

____

Are there more alcoholics than drug addicts? Circle YES or NO...

The answer is YES.

Alcoholics have many places to go for inexpensive help. Are alcoholics less of a threat to the fabric of our society than drug addicts? Circle YES or NO...

Or are they both sad and lost individuals who need help? Circle YES or NO...

“Did you know that the first large scale importer of cocaine and heroin into the United States was the CIA,” Vent said. “They were funding revolutionary groups in both the Middle East and South and Central America?

Do you think this is true? Circle YES or NO...

The answer is YES.

Do you think the CIA still dabbles in illegal trade to accomplish its agenda?

Circle YES or NO...

If you answered NO are you positive? Circle YES or NO...

Do you think the CIA should be able to break the law? A space for your answer:

____

____

Did you know that since Portugal legalized possession of all narcotics drug use has gone down? Circle YES or NO...

The answer is YES. A space for your ideas on why drug use went down:

____

____

Could it be the same reasons tobacco use has gone down even though tobacco is legal? Circle YES or NO...

Australia, the Netherlands, and the Czech Republic have also legalized the possession of drugs. These countries seem to be doing fine. Could it be that putting drug users in jail is in all reality a government's way of control. Circle YES or NO...

"William," Vent said, "What do you think about religious organizations getting involved with politics?"

"I was always under the understanding that the founding fathers did not want church and state to have anything to do with each other," I replied truthfully.

"I think politicians are courting churches now," Vent said. "It is a highly manipulative voter base."

Did you know that white Christians have declined in the United States to only about 40%? Circle YES or NO...

The answer is YES.

Did you know younger people are less and less likely to be religious? Circle YES or NO...

The answer is YES.

In time will this effect politics? Circle YES or NO...your reasoning:

____

____

Do you think religion should be involved in politics? Circle YES or NO...a space for your reasoning:

____

____

If religion has a place in politics then should churches be taxed? Circle your answer YES or NO...your reasoning:

Steve Furtick has an evangelical flock of 14,000 people and owns a 16,000 square foot home in Weddington, N.C. He proclaims the house is a gift from God and his congregation agrees. Is his house a gift from God? Circle YES or NO...should he have to pay taxes? Circle YES or NO...

Joel Osteen from Texas, pastor of over 43,000 believers, has one house valued at ten million dollars and a smaller house worth three million dollars. His many books draw advances of close to ten million each. Should good old boy Joel have to pay taxes? Circle YES or NO...or does God like him a lot more than he likes the average person that goes to his church? Circle YES or NO...

If the majority of people feel churches should not have to pay taxes I am going to start a church. It will be called BOB'S CHURCH THAT DOES NOT PAY TAXES. I will preach greed is good, charity is a weakness, bigotry is the natural order of life, and Rock and Roll music was invented by God. I will build a huge church the size of the Super Bowl Stadium because having an expensive place of worship means God is on my side. I will buy a two million dollar home because my congregation believes God wanted me to have it. I will wear gold jewelry, expensive suits, hand made shoes, my teeth will be capped, and I will have my fingernails manicured. I will buy a jet and tell people all over the world the only reason people are poor is because they are lazy and do not have enough grit to put money in my collection plate.

"I have to tell you something you might not like," I informed Vent. "I think you enjoyed your life more when life's absurdities made you jerk around like you had fleas."

"You cannot tell but my insides are doing summersaults and back flips over the topics we discuss," Vent admitted.

I didn't reply but inwardly I miss the arm tossing and twitching of Vent when I first met him.

"What do you think about having term limits for Congress?" I asked.

Vent made a face like congress was something so rotten even catfish would not eat it.

To lighten things up for a moment I have a friend in Missouri who catches catfish using Ivory soap for bait. All you people who fish for catfish did you know Ivory soap is good catfish bait? Circle YES or NO...

Do you know that catfish was one of the first commercially farmed fish in the United States. Circle YES or NO...

Do you know that the majority of catfish you buy at the supermarket now comes from Asian fish farms? Circle YES or NO...

Also, the majority of shrimp comes from Asian shrimp farms.

In the United States carp fish are considered a trash fish and are normally caught and tossed up on the bank. In Europe they are considered a game fish and delicious.

Why is this? Your answer:

____

____

If you are ever in Omaha, Nebraska there are several restaurants that specialize in serving carp fish. Try it. It is very good when cooked correctly.

Back to the stinking congress. Do you think that congress should be limited to two terms exactly like the president? Circle YES or NO...explain your reasoning:

____

____

Congress stated that a president who is in office too long can become easy to manipulate and overcome with power? Is this true? Circle YES or NO...

If you believe it is true then why doesn't congress have term limits? Circle one or more: I DON'T KNOW...THEY ARE SMART...WE THE PUBLIC ARE STUPID...and a space for your reasoning:

____

____

Contrary to popular belief members of congress are covered by the same health insurance the normal citizen has (this was passed by President Obama) which Trump will most likely overturn. They can retire at 50 but have to serve more than one term. The base retirement is around $75,000 and the yearly income is $174,000 for working less than half of a year. Their income gets a yearly cost of living index and they do pay Social Security. They also receive a stipend for travel and others costs that pertain to their work. Members of Congress are by law not allowed to accept money from special interest groups. Do you think members of congress do not accept special interest money? Circle YES or NO...

If you answered NO how do so many congressmen become millionaires while they are in office? Your answer:

____

____

Why is accepting millions of dollars from special interests groups for reelection not considered taking money? A space for your reasoning:

____

____

Also, if they supposedly do not take money while in office are they given special consideration by special interest groups after they retire? Circle YES or NO...

Do you think Congressmen really and truly feel they work for the American people? Circle YES or NO...

Or are they more like Kings and Queens ruling the ill-informed mob? Circle YES or NO...

Many members of the Senate and Congress after they retire begin working for Washington D.C. lobbying firms - another great example of the government working for themselves and not the people.

Do you think retired government employees should be able to work for lobbying firms? Circle your answer YES or NO...

A question? The United States rebelled against the British over taxes and the fact the British government really did not care a tea bag for the American rabble. If this is true then why do United States Judges (state, federal, supreme court) all wear long black robes like the British did and still do? Is it because our government has become like the British? Circle your answer YES or NO...

I will say at least the United States Judges do not wear those stupid looking wigs the British lawyers and judges do. Do you think wearing a wig when you are a judge makes you feel superior or more like a fool? Circle SUPERIOR or FOOL...no need for a space. In my opinion anyone who is a judge or wants to be a judge is a person who would have done much better in life minding their own business. One day computers will be judges and we will not be shackled by human judgments or prejudices. The law will be the law and not open to interpretation. Do you think computers would make better judges? Circle YES or NO...and a space for your reasoning:

____

____

If you were a black person on trial for possession of drugs would you rather have a computer for a judge or twelve white men? Circle COMPUTER or TWELVE WHITE MEN...

If you were a white man on trial for killing a black man would you feel slightly intimidated if the jury was composed of all black people and the judge was black? Circle YES or NO...

Do you think that black people receive fair trials from all white juries? Circle YES or NO...

Not exactly a judge question but why are police officers rarely convicted of murder or manslaughter when video evidence clearly shows otherwise?

____

____

If you shot an unarmed person 16 or 20 times do you think you would beat the murder or manslaughter charge? Circle YES or NO...

If you shot someone in the back four times while they were running away would you beat the murder or manslaughter charge by saying you feared for your life? Circle YES or NO...

Do you think if cops keep killing people more people will start killing cops?

Circle YES or NO...

A strange fact but 2017 had fewer police being shot and killed than in the last ten years.

Vent finished his beer and held up the empty glass for the bartender to see. I finished mine and also held up my glass.

"Do you know what country brews the most beer?" Vent asked.

"It has to be a European country," I replied.

Vent shook his head. "No, China brews more beer than any other country in the world with the United States being the second largest brewer of beer."

Were you surprised China is the largest brewer of beer? Circle YES or NO...

Maybe we have more in common with the Chinese than we think. I wonder since there are so many beer drinkers in China if they secretly wish to own pickup trucks. What do you think? Circle YES or NO...

"The number one selling beer in the world is Snow Beer made in China. The company is partially owned by Miller," Vent said. "They do not bother to export it they make so much money."

I was amazed.

"The world consumes over 35 billion gallons of beer each year and by volume beer is cheaper to buy than bottled water," Vent stated.

"A lot of countries you can't drink the water but you can drink the beer," I said.

"The water they use to make the beer is the water you can't drink," Vent said with an ironic grin. "Even though it is boiled it is still the same water."

The next time you are drinking a Corona, or a beer from Vietnam, or other parts of the Orient think about the above statement. There are many people who have seen the rivers in the Orient. The rivers there are not sparkling clear water. If you go to Mexico only idiots drink the water. Let me give you a tip, this also means ice unless it is made from bottled water.

"I wonder if more people drink wine than beer," I said.

"Wine is the second most consumed alcohol product," Vent replied.

Do you know what country drinks the most wine per-capita in the world? I will give you a hint it is not France. A space for your guess:

____

It is those sneaky Catholics in Vatican City, Italy.

Setting the beers down the bartender said, "I couldn't help but overhear your conversation, some of the topics caught my interest."

"What is something that you find ridiculous or bothers you?" I asked the bartender.

The bartender seemed surprised. The majority of bartenders are never asked their opinion on matters. Their job is to listen patiently while you go on and on about your own problems while never taking into consideration the bartender must have problems of his own. Think about this. Have you ever gone into a bar and even before you ordered a drink the bartender started telling you his problems. Circle YES or NO...

"Before you start," I said to the bartender. "What is your name?"

"Frank," he replied with a slight hesitation. Organized crime figures are not into the habit of telling people their last name – it makes them uncomfortable.

"Tell me something that bothers you," I said.

"When a man gets out of jail, supposedly having satisfied his commitment to society, he cannot own a weapon," Frank said.

"Many states do have a process where felons can apply to get their gun rights back, it takes time and money, but it is there," Vent said.

"I didn't know that," Frank replied in surprise.

Do you believe that a felon who has served his time should be able to purchase a weapon? Circle YES or NO...a space for your reasoning:

____

____

If you answered NO should a person arrested for marijuana possession, petty theft, or many other slight offences when they are young be cursed by their crime for their entire life? Circle YES or NO...

If you answered NO what does HAVING SERVED THEIR COMMITMENT TO SOCIETY mean? Circle I DON'T KNOW or NOTHING....or a space for you to explain what it means:

____

____

"What is the percentage of bad or crooked cops?" Vent asked Frank.

"All cops are bad in my opinion," Frank said adding with a dry smile, "but I am in a profession that is not exactly cop friendly."

"I am not a big fan of cops myself," Vent said. "I know they are necessary but giving someone too much power has a way of changing them in a negative way."

"Does your question mean all cops including Border Patrol, State Police, Sheriffs Departments, FBI, and CIA?" I asked.

"All the departments," Vent said.

"10% are crooked," I guessed.

"Actually by statistics about 1% of all police officers are crooked, but about 15% know how to use the law to their advantage, often pushing the limits of the law to the maximum," Vent said.

Do you think only 1% of cops are crooked? Circle YES or NO...

If you were a cop and a major crime organization offered you $250,000 to look the other way would you take the money? Circle YES or NO...

If you were a cop and a major crime organization gave you a choice you could work for them or have your wife, parents, or children killed would you work for them? Circle YES or NO...

"What is the percentage of people who don't trust the police?" Vent asked. Circle your answer: 10%...25%...50%...75% or 100%.

"No one I know trusts the police," Frank said.

The answer is about 56% do not trust the police. In minority communities it is 95%.

Do you trust the police? Circle YES or NO...a space for your reasoning:

____

____

"What percentage of cops are racists?" Frank asked.

"That would be hard to know," Vent said. "A cop isn't going to say he hates black people or brown people or white people and keep his job. But it is known that during a normal year 25% of people shot by police are black, 18% to 20% are Hispanics, there is always a few Asians, and the rest are white – white being Italians, Greeks, Irish, Jews, and all the other races that live in America."

Are those percentages surprising to you? Circle YES or NO...

Do you think Black Lives Matter is a racist organization? Circle your answer YES or NO...and a space for your reasoning:

____

____

For years organized crime has placed some of their members in police forces. Do you think this was smart on their part or not? Circle your answer SMART...NOT SMART...your reasoning:

____

The FBI states many hate groups have positioned people in various police forces.

Do you think this is smart on their part or not: Circle your answer SMART...NOT SMART...

During the Civil Rights Movement over 50% of police in the south were members of the KKK. Is this true? Circle YES or NO...

The answer is NO. 35% of the police were members of the KKK.

I will ask you once again. Do you trust cops? Circle YES or NO...

Here is a simple question? If you had your life to do all over again would you want to be a cop? Circle YES or NO...

"That is enough conversation about cops for me," Frank said and went to do whatever bartenders do when they are tired of conversation.

For some reason Vent started to chuckle. "I don't see where talking about cops is a funny matter?" I said.

"I just had a passing thought about alternative facts," he said.

"I don't think alternative facts are funny either. The fact our fearless leader lives by them is disheartening to say the least."

What would happen if you told your boss alternative facts about why the report you were supposed to have was late? Circle your answer: YOU WOULD GET FIRED...NOTHING WOULD HAPPEN YOUR BOSS IS A LIAR...

What would happen if you told a judge alternative facts? Circle your answer: THE JUDGE WOULD LET YOU GO FREE...THE JUDGE WOULD LAUGH... THE JUDGE WOULD TOSS YOUR LYING BUTT IN JAIL...

What would happen if you filled out a job application with alternative facts?

Circle your answer: YOU WOULD GET HIRED...YOUR APPLICATION WOULD BE TOSSED IN THE GARBAGE...

Why can a politician lie and people don't seem to care? Circle your answer: THE PUBLIC IS STUPID...THE PUBLIC DOES NOT CARE...THE PUBLIC IS DEAF...and a space for your answer:

____

____

Why is it when a person is sworn in for jury duty or to testify in court they are made to repeat, 'I solemnly swear to tell the truth and nothing but the truth,' when most of the time everyone knows they are going to lie. Circle your answer: PEOPLE DON'T CARE WHAT THE TRUTH IS...LYING IS NORMAL...LYING IS ACCEPTABLE BEHAVIOR AND SHOULD BE TAUGHT TO ALL OF OUR CHILDREN SO THEY GROW UP TO BE JUST LIKE THE MAJORITY OF OUR LEADERS.

If you believe in alternative facts, is it then true, you can never call anybody a liar? Circle your answer YES or NO.

What is the difference between alternative facts and the truth? A space for your answer:

____

____

What is the difference between alternative facts and a lie? Your answer:

____

____

When George Washington told his father the story concerning the Cherry Tree was he lying or using alternative facts? Circle your answer: LYING...ALTERNATIVE FACTS...

In my day and age I do know one thing for sure. If I would have told either my mother or father alternative facts I would have not enjoyed the consequences.

If someone lied to you all the time would you trust them? Circle your answer YES or NO...

If you would trust liars I want you to lend me $100,000. I promise I will pay you back double within six months. No lie, really, $200,000 for only $100,000 and all you have to do is trust me for six months.

I noticed Vent's beer was almost finished. "Julia would like you to come to dinner tonight. I have beer at the house," I said.

"You have met a lady you like," Vent smiled.

"I more than like her," I replied. "She has given me a sense of well being that I have never experienced before."

"Have you told her you love her?" Vent asked.

"I think both of us are apprehensive to take that next step," I replied.

"I would enjoy meeting Julia and eating at your house," Vent said. "Then when we are done you could take me to my hotel."

Vent started to reach for his billfold. "No on me," I said in a way there was no room for argument.

Frank brought the bill and said to Vent, "I like you, you get into any trouble while you are in town have William let me know."

Vent shook hands with Frank. "I take that as a compliment," he said.

As we neared the car Vent remarked, "It never hurts to know a few characters from the other side of life. It is a sad truth but many people only understand force and fear."

Is it true that many people only understand force and fear? Circle YES or NO...

For people who only understand force or fear is kindness even an option? Circle YES or NO...

Rush hour traffic was at its finest with six lanes of bumper to bumper traffic going twenty miles an hour over the speed limit. "10,000,000 people live within 50 square miles of here," I stated.

"Evangelical groups and the government want to stop Planned Parenthood," Vent said calmly, but then his arms shot out from his sides, he started to shake, his eyes rolled around in their sockets, and he shouted, "What in the hell do they think they are doing?

It was good to see Vent become Vent again.

"Did you now that in the United States 1 in 6 people have food insecurity which is the lack of access to enough food for a family member?" Vent asked. Circle YES or NO...

"There are 42 million Americans living in poverty," Vent continued.

Why in the United States is there so much poverty? A space for your answer:

____

____

If we cannot feed the people that are alive today how are we going to feed a growing population? Your answer:

____

____

There are over 400,000 children in the Foster Home Program in the United States. Over 100,000 of these are waiting to be adopted. Why is it that all the people who are against Planned Parenthood and abortion have not adopted six or seven children? A space for your answer:

____

____

Is it because they think God will solve the problem? Circle your answer YES or NO...

Is it because they are hypocrites? Circle your answer YES or NO...

Did you know that there are no longer orphanages in the United States? Circle your answer

YES or NO...

The answer is YES there are no orphanages in the United States.

Would the return to the orphanage system be better than farming children out to private foster families who get paid to take care of the children until they are adopted? Circle your answer YES or NO...

Did you know there are over 500,000 children in Foster Care? Circle YES or NO...

The answer is YES.

Did you know that more children in the United States have been killed by family members in the last ten years than combat deaths for our military personnel in the Middle East and Afghanistan? Circle YES or NO...

The answer is YES.

What percentages of Foster Children are abused while in foster care? Circle your answer: 5%...10%...20%...30%...

The answer is between 5% and 10%.

Vent stopped waving his arms around and once again took on the demeanor of a calm and clear headed English Professor. "How many orphans do you think there are in the world?" he asked. Circle your answer: 10,000...50,000...75,000...125,000...250,000... 1,000,000...and a space if you think none of these are correct: _______________

"There are over 10,000,000 orphans in the world," Vent said.

"Very sad," I said.

"Why are people against Planned Parenthood if they are not going to take care of unwanted children?" Vent asked. Your answer:

"Overall the human race is not a great attribute to our planet," Vent said.

Do you think the human race is a great attribute to the planet? Circle your answer YES or NO...your reasoning either way.

For either of your answers here are a few questions to ponder: Are there any other species on the earth that pollute? Circle YES or NO...

The answer is NO.

Are there any other creatures that have the potential of destroying the planet? Circle YES or NO...

The answer is NO.

Are there any other creatures that feel a need to attend church? Circle YES or NO...

The answer is NO.

Are there any other creatures that will kill each other over a doctrine that cannot be proven by any tangible means except faith? Circle YES or NO...

The answer is NO.

Are there any other creatures that kill other creatures merely for the sport of it? Circle YES or NO...

The answer is YES. Cats kill for sport.

Are there any other creatures that need money? Circle YES or NO...

The answer is NO.

Are there any other creatures that want to conquer the world? Circle YES or NO...

The answer is NO.

Are there any other creatures that want to enslave other creatures? Circle YES or NO...

The answer is NO.

Are there any other creatures that hate other creatures simply because they are different from them? YES or NO...

The answer is NO.

Are there any other creatures that believe in heaven and hell? Circle YES or NO...

The answer is NO.

The Pope recently said pets will go to heaven. Do you believe this? Circle YES or NO...

If pets can go to heaven then does it mean all animals have souls? Circle YES or NO...

Or does it mean only certain animals have souls? Circle YES or NO...

If your answer was YES what certain animals have souls? A space for your answer

____

____

Does a creature need a soul to get into heaven? Your reasoning:

____

____

Julia was in the kitchen. The aroma of Mexican food filled the air. I hoped she was cooking her baked red cheese enchiladas. They are delicious.

Julia, without being introduced, hugged Vent. "William has nothing but good things to say about you," she said with an expansive smile.

"It is my pleasure to meet you," Vent replied sincerely.

"Would you like a beer? We have Corona, or a mixed drink, we have rum, vodka, or gin. I make a killer martini."

"Beer would be fine, but I would enjoy one of your martinis after dinner," Vent said.

I opened three beers. "To what ever makes us not go crazy," I toasted.

"And what keeps you from going crazy?" Julia asked Vent.

"I am afraid it is too late," Vent replied. "I have been crazy for many years."

Do you believe the statement a wealthy person is eccentric but a poor person is crazy is true? Circle YES or NO...

Do you know the definition of crazy? A space for your explanation:

____

Crazy, according to the dictionary means: brainsick, demented, disturbed, mad, sick, unbalanced, and unhinged. But it also states that the adjective crazy should be used to describe actions that aren't sensible: crazy love, the clown was crazy, he is football crazy. It also states that using the word crazy for a person who is insane can be considered offensive and hurtful.

"What do you think is crazy in our modern world?" Vent asked Julia.

"War and greed are crazy," she replied.

Do you think war is crazy? Circle YES or NO...

Is some of the craziness taken out of war when a country is attacked and has to defend itself? Circle YES or NO...

Seems to me the many wars the United States has fought since World War II have had nothing to do with us being attacked. Am I right or wrong with this assumption? Circle RIGHT or WRONG.

"I think Portland, Oregon's annual naked bicycle parade is crazy," I commented.

"You would think it would hurt," Vent grimaced. "But there are hundreds of participants."

"I think it would be fun to watch," Julia said.

Would you ride a bicycle naked through a large metropolitan city just for the hell of it? Circle YES or NO...and a space for your reasoning either way:

Do you think it would hurt? Circle YES or NO...

“What do you think about the group of women that have started a movement to legalize women going topless?” Vent asked Julia.

“They have not reached the saggy breast age yet,” Julia laughed. “And I feel there are far more important women’s issues than going topless.”

“Unequal pay is one,” Vent said.

Julia nodded with a disgusted look on her face.

“Very little time off for maternity leave is another,” Vent said.

“Things are slowly changing,” Julia said, “but I don’t know if our government is forward thinking enough to catch up with the rest of the world.”

“In Finland a mother receives a total of 25 weeks of maternity leave. In Denmark the mother gets 18 weeks of maternity leave and after that the parents can split 32 weeks of leave however they see fit. In Sweden the parents receive 480 days of maternity leave of which the father gets 90 with guaranteed pay. In Belgium the mother gets 15 weeks of maternity leave at 75% of her salary. In Iceland the parents get 9 months of maternity leave split down the middle for father and mother. In Norway mothers can take 35 weeks of maternity leave at full pay or 45 weeks and 80%. In Hungary mothers get 70% of their pay for 24 weeks. Mothers in Estonia are given 140 full paid days of maternity leave,” Vent informed us, adding, “The United States is the only government in the free world that does not have a federal law concerning maternity leave.”

Do you think women should be able to stay home from work and nurture their children for a period of time with pay? Circle YES or NO...and a space for your reasoning:

____

If you answered NO is a person's job more important than their family? Circle YES or NO...

At the same time I am writing this book Congress is in a deadlock if a woman should get two weeks off for maternity leave. At the moment men are not under consideration. I guess if women receive two fully paid weeks off after having a baby the entire economy will go in the tank and every company will go bankrupt. Companies will then stop hiring women because they will say they are a drain on productivity.

Do you think two weeks off for maternity leave is too much? Circler YES or NO...a space for your reasoning:

____

____

Do you think women deserve the same pay as men for the same job? Circle YES or NO...your reasoning either way:

____

____

If you answered YES why do women receive less pay for the same job?

If your answer was NO, why should women be paid less?

Has the United States put capitalism above the needs of the people? Circle YES or NO...

Does the United States respect the needs of a corporation or business above the needs of normal workers? Circle YES or NO...

If you answered NO why are the rich growing richer and the middle class and below are getting poorer? Your answer:

If a CEO of a major corporation was paid 200 million dollars instead of 300 million dollars and the extra 100 million dollars was given to the workers would the life style of the CEO change in anyway? Circle YES or NO...

Would the life styles of the workers change by getting a raise? Circle YES or NO...

If the workers life styles would not change drastically would the extra money at least give them a little peace of mind? Circle YES or NO...

Why don't most businesses want their workers to be comfortable?

____

____

The United States fearless leader is always spouting off about the United States losing jobs to foreign workers and yet his daughter's businesses have their products made overseas? Am I missing something here? Circle YES or NO...

Also, the president has many of his products made overseas.

Has anyone heard a Trump supporter say anything negative about the above statement? Circle YES or NO...

"Did you know that Missouri lowered the minimum wage?" Vent stated.

"Why would they do that?" I asked.

"The governor stated by lowering the minimum wage more business would move to Missouri," Vent said.

Do you think this is true? Circle YES or NO...

"Minimum wage is a crime," Vent said.

I did not comment on the statement, knowing it is true, and knowing anyone who is against raising the minimum wage has never tried to exist on one. There is a pamphlet that was recently published explaining how to live on a minimum wage job. If you are interested you can find it on the internet. The only thing it forgets to list is a food allotment. I take it poor people do not have to eat

There are many people who say raising the minimum wage hurts small businesses. Do you think this is true: Circle YES or NO...

Is raising the minimum wage a double edged sword? Circle YES or NO...

Large companies received tax incentives from states. Why isn't some of that money given to the workers? Your answer:

____

____

If two people are working for minimum wage can they afford to buy a house? Circle YES or NO...your reasoning:

____

____

Can they afford to buy a descent car? Circle YES or NO...Why or Why Not?

____

____

If businesses paid a living wage would it reduce the need for food stamps and welfare? Circle

YES or NO...

If it would reduce the need for food stamps and welfare wouldn't the government save money? Circle YES or NO...

If the government saved money would your taxes go down? Circle YES or NO...

Have taxes ever gone down? Circle YES or NO...

The answer is NO. If they go down in one area they are always raised in another.

If the individual states and the federal government decided to lower the minimum wage to $5.00 do you think businesses would continue to pay what they are mandated to pay now? Circle YES or NO...

If companies lowered wages do you think they would lower product cost to the public? Circle YES or NO...or...would they reap more profit? Circle YES or NO...

A space for your reasoning:

____

____

There was an article in an established news magazine (which some people now call fake news) where rich people in Seattle were complaining that since the minimum wage has been raised they could only afford to go out to eat three times a week. It almost made me cry. Do you feel sorry for rich people who can only go out to eat three times a week? Circle YES or NO...

A timer went off in the kitchen. "Time to eat," Julia announced. "If you don't like red enchiladas you are out of luck."

Vent did not say a word while he ate. After eating five enchiladas he leaned back in his chair obviously pleased. “Devine,” he said. “I love Mexican food.”

“Would you like a martini now?” Julia asked.

“I think I have died and somehow made it to heaven,” Vent said which both Julia and I knew meant he would really enjoy a martini.

“Gin or vodka?” Julia asked.

“I never was a big fan of the British, vodka please,” Vent said.

“I’ll have another beer,” I said.

Without hesitation Julia replied, “You know where the refrigerator is, this is your apartment and I am not your maid.”

Vent chuckled.

“That’s why I like you so much,” I said to Julia.

She blew me a kiss.

“What do you have against the British?” I asked Vent.

“Nothing against the people but the adoration for royalty has always seemed strange to me. A family takes control of a country by power, subjugates the majority of the people, taxes them to death, builds huge castles and estates all over the land, invades other countries and the people love them for keeping them poor. God save the Queen and all that rot,” Vent said with a wry grin.

“It does seem slightly strange,” I agreed.

Do you give a hoot about the Queen of England? Circle YES or NO.

Did you know that the Queen is one of the richest women in the world? Circle YES or NO...For that matter do you really care what happens in Britain? Circle YES or NO...

With the way the United States is now would you rather live in Britain?

Circle YES or NO...

They do have universal healthcare, good beer, and fish and chips. But the weather has a lot to be desired and since Britain has decided to leave the European Union they are in as much turmoil as the United States. Their government feels that by standing alone they can make better deals in the world market than by combining buying and selling possibilities with over twenty other nations. Seems to me it would be like a Mom and Pop store thinking they can compete with Walmart.

Can a Mom and Pop store compete with Walmart? Circle YES or NO...

According to our esteemed President the United States is going to start standing alone. Does this mean we should stop importing foreign cars? Circle YES or NO...

Should we stop importing anything from China? Circle YES or NO...

Should we stop importing anything from Canada? Circle YES or NO...

Should we stop importing food from Mexico and Central America? Circle YES or NO...

Should it be illegal to own any vehicle or product that was not made in the

United States? Circle YES or NO...

If we stopped importing goods could the United States take care of itself? Circle YES or NO...your reasoning:

____

____

One good thing might happen if we stopped importing items it would be hard for the United

States to keep sticking its nose in other countries business.

Does it seem to you that the United States has developed a very, very, very, long nose? Circle YES or NO...

It has been kept out of the news but since the crack down on Mexican immigrants many crops are not getting picked in California and Texas. Also many fishing and shrimp boats are short handed.

The farmers and boat owners say white people won't apply for the jobs.

Why aren't white people applying for the jobs? Circle your answer: THEY ARE RICH...THEY FEEL COMMON WORK IS BELOW THEM...THEY FEEL SUPERIOR TO OTHER RACES...THEY ARE ON WELFARE AND FOODSTAMPS...THEY THINK THE PAY IS NOT ENOUGH...a space for any reasons you can think of:

____

____

If immigrants are stealing our jobs what jobs are they stealing? Your list of jobs:

____

____

Why is it that people who hire illegal aliens are not prosecuted and put in jail? A space for your answer:

____

____

If you really want to stop illegal immigration every company that hires an illegal immigrant should be fined ½ of their gross value. An individual that hires an illegal maid or gardener should be fined ½ the value of their home or property. There can only be illegal immigration if companies and people will hire them. If there are no jobs then there will be no illegal immigration. Do you believe this is true? Circle YES or NO...

Over 60% of people working in Trump Hotels have temporary worker permits.

Does this seem funny? Trump would not need temporary workers if American citizens would take the jobs.

What do you think could be done to curb illegal immigration? Your answer:

____

____

An interesting fact. Since Trump dropped out of the Trans Pacific Trade Union eleven nations have made their own agreement completely ignoring the United States. The Trans Pacific Trade Union composes 20% of all world trade. Is the good or bad for the United States? Circle YES or NO...your reasoning:

____

"The man who invented the martini was a genius," Vent said after taking a sip. "He made it fashionable to drink two shots of liquor at a time and not seem like a lush."

"I have an elderly lady friend who drinks Old Fashions," Julia said. "Whenever we get together she drinks two or three and never seems to get tipsy. For some reason I thought Old Fashions were no stronger than drinking iced tea. One evening I asked if I could taste her drink. Was I surprised? I had no idea there are two shots of whiskey in an Old Fashion. My friend laughed and said, "Old Fashions are a way for a lady to drink whisky and seem classy."

For all you rough and tumble whiskey drinkers out there if you drink six shots of whiskey that is the equivalent to three Old Fashions. Can you drink six shots of whiskey without slurring your words? Circle YES or NO...

If you answered NO Julia knows an elderly lady that can drink you under the table. Did you know that the cocktail was invented during prohibition when most of the illegal booze tasted terrible? Smuggled booze from Canada, Mexico, Europe, and South America tastes the same as it does now.

"What is America's favorite cocktail?" Vent asked.

"Rum and Coke," I guessed.

"Bloody Mary," Julia said.

"The Martini and the Old Fashion are always neck and neck in popularity," Vent answered.

"I don't want to offend you Vent," Julia said, "but from what William told me about you I was expecting to meet a person who could not sit down he was so agitated with the world and when you talked your words shot out as fast as angry hornets."

"As I told William I have changed my image plus if I get agitated or animated to much I am prone to mild depression," Vent said.

"What depresses you the most?" Julia asked.

"The dumbing down of America," Vent said as a slight tremor swept through his body making his face twitch and his eyebrows arch. "It seems over the past several years some force has swept over the nation that makes people proud to have no common sense or a true grasp of life."

Do you think because a person does not have an education they are dumb? Circle YES or NO...a space for your reasoning:

____

____

Do you think because a person does not have an education they also do not have common sense? Circle YES or NO...your reasoning:

____

____

Could the dumbing down of America include educated people? Circle YES or NO...and a space for your reasoning:

Most of our leaders are highly educated but when it comes to running the country they seem to be pretty dumb. Do you agree with this statement? Circle YES or NO...

Neither my grandmother nor my grandfather graduated from high school. They purchased a small farm in Iowa when they were first married, which they sold later in life, and opened a combination bar and restaurant in a small town. They lived through the depression and World War II. They both possessed more common sense than any other person I have met in my lifetime. They educated themselves by reading and debating both sides of any topic. They were also in many ways not your true blue bible belters as they did not believe in the Japanese American Internment camps during the war, the dropping of fire bombs and the atomic bomb on civilians, the purging of people Hoover thought were communist, the policy of segregation, and believed women should be treated the same way as men. They also thought the United States was taking the same path as the Roman Empire and one day would fall.

Do you think the United States is following the same path to destruction as the Roman Empire? Circle YES or NO...and space for your reasoning:

If you answered NO do you believe that the United States will always be a world power? Circle

YES or NO...your reasoning:

____

____

China has been a country for over 2,000 years and the United States as of 2017 has been a country for 241years. Do you think China looks at the United States like America is an adolescent who really has no idea what the real world is all about but instead lives in a fantasy of grandeur and beliefs that the rest of the world idolizes them? Circle YES or NO...space for your reasoning either way:

____

____

What country has the largest economy in the world China or the United States? Circle CHINA or UNITED STATES...

The answer is China.

Which has the greatest buying power – the Chinese middle class or the United States middle class? Circle CHINA or UNITED STATES...

China is the answer.

Do you think it might be a good idea to learn Chinese? Circle YES or NO....

This might be hard as many people in the United States barely speak English.

99% of the Chinese people, even rural, speak two languages.

“How many people are there in the United States that cannot read?” Vent asked.

“There couldn’t be many,” I replied.

“According to the Department of Education 32,000,000 people in the United States cannot read, 21% of adults in the United States read below the 5th grade level, and 19% of high school graduates can’t comprehend what they read. Alarming as these statistics are the worst thing about it is most of these people can vote,” Vent said.

Do you think a person who votes should be able to read? Circle YES or NO....your reasoning:

____

____

“With the way the federal government and the state governments keep cutting back on funding for education I can’t see the situation stopping any day soon,” I said.

“The government in all reality wants more ill informed people voting than those who understand what is going on,” Vent said.

Do you think the above statement is true? Circle TRUE or FALSE...your reasoning:

____

____

Do you think politicians call the news outlets spreaders of fake news because they want to control the news? Circle YES or NO...

Do you think the major news outlets fabricate news? Circle YES or NO...

If you answered YES why would they make up fake news? Your answer:

____

____

Do you think that curtailing the news is the first step toward a totalitarian government? Circle YES or NO...your reasoning:

____

____

When George Washington was President he stopped taking the Philadelphia newspaper because he thought it spread lies about him.

If you believe newspapers and other media outlets should only be able to report what the government gives them permission to you should move to Russia or China or North Korea.

Would you like to live permanently in Russia? Circle YES or NO...

Would you like to live permanently in China? Circle YES or NO...

Would you like to live permanently in North Korea? Circle YES or NO...

If you answered YES to any of the above questions here is a space to explain why:

If you did answer YES, like my grandfather use to say, "Don't let the door hit you in the ass."

"What do you think about charter schools?" Julia asked Vent.

Vent thought a few moments before he replied. "Both public and charter schools are free to attend and neither can discriminate students because of race, gender, or disability. Both public and charter schools get their funding from the state, which is from your taxes, and must comply with the state guidelines for education. Charter schools differ from public schools as the majority are operated for profit. Unlike pubic schools students must apply to the charter school they wish to attend. What I disagree with is if the charter school is funded by the state why are they allowed to be profit making for a company and not the state? By giving money to profit making charter schools you are taking money away from public schools. By taking money away from public schools you are taking money away from schools in lower income areas that need financial help the most."

"A private school differs from a charter school in the fact a private school receives no state funding," I said. "They can teach what they wish. Private Catholic Schools teach Catholic doctrine. Private Baptist Schools teach Baptist doctrine and on and on. One problem about private schools is the average cost is $19,000 a year, which is out of the range for about 95% of the country."

Do you believe that a charter school, which is funded by your tax dollars, should be allowed to make money for private investors? Circle YES or NO...

If you do I am going to open a fast food establishment and call it Charter Eats. Your tax dollars will buy my inventory and pay the bills for my overhead but I will keep all of the profit and then if I go out of business you will be stuck with the bill. It seems like a good deal to me.

"The government is trying to implement charter schools because they do not want the responsibility of public schools," I said.

"The modern Republican wants fewer government sanctions on any business," Vent said.

Do you think if business is in control and not the government there will be more jobs? Circle YES or NO...

How can there be more jobs when there is the same number of businesses either run by the government or the private sector? Your answer:

____

____

Do you think that big business needs oversight? Circle YES or NO...

If you answered NO you had better research working conditions before the unions managed to intervene.

Now there is a big push to get rid of unions and also government oversight.

I have asked this question in a different form earlier. Do you think that the majority of politicians both Republican and Democrat are working for big business? Circle your answer YES or NO...

If they are not working for big business who are they working for? A space for who you think they work for:

____

____

If you said the American People, sorry to say, I strongly disagree.

"Would you make me another martini," Vent asked Julia.

"Two is your limit," Julia said in a way Vent knew there was no room for argument.

Here is a random question. Do you worry about what is happening to the Pacific Ocean from all the radiation that is still leaking from the reactor melt down in Japan? Circle YES or NO...

Have you even thought about it? Circle YES or NO...

There have been reports that the radiation has reached the west coast of the United States. There are also reports that the radiation levels are not high enough to cause harm to marine life. Do you think this is true? Circle YES or NO...

If you think it is true why do people administering x-rays stand behind a lead screen when you get low radiation x-rays? Your reasoning:

____

____

Is any level of radiation good for you? Circle YES or NO...

"Recently I have noticed there has been no mention in the news concerning the number of casualties the United States has been inflicting on civilians in Syria and Iraq with the increase of our bombing on these countries," I said.

Vent's eyes darted from side to side for a moment. With extreme effort he stopped them. "The military estimates American forces have killed slightly over 300 civilians since 2014 in Iraq and Syria. Airwars, which is a non-profit organization that tracks civilian casualties in Iraq and Syria, states the United States has killed close to 3,000 civilians. This does not count wounded," Vent said.

"I suppose it is the price of war," Julia said pragmatically as she handed Vent his martini.

"The price of war," Vent repeated. "Death, destruction, mayhem, cruelty, insanity, carnage, are all the price of war. Is there a good price of war?" Vent asked.

Do you think there is there a good price of war? Circle YES or NO...and a space for you to list a few good prices of war if you answered YES:

____

____

There are many people who benefit from war. I will name a few, weapons companies, the Pentagon, gun powder producers, Halliburton: Can you to name a few?

____

____

If I was attempting to kill my enemies by bombing your city but killed your wife and children by mistake would you seek vengeance? Circle YES or NO...if you answered YES here you can explain how you would seek vengeance:

___

___

If your family was killed by American forces would you do anything in your power to kill Americans? Circle YES or NO...

Or, if your family was killed by American forces would you just shrug your shoulders and say, "Civilian casualties are the price of war." Circle YES or NO...

Merely for your information and something to ponder: 7,000,000 civilians were killed in WWI. 50,000,000 civilians were killed in WWII. 600,000 civilians were killed in Korea. 2,000,000 civilians were killed in Vietnam. 500,000 civilians have been killed so far in Iraq and last but not least 26,000 civilians have been killed in Afghanistan.

Over 3,000 civilians have been killed in Syria by coalition air strikes and over 400,000 civilians have been killed so far during the war. These figures do not include wounded civilians or those affected by famine due to war. The ongoing conflicts in Africa, which the United States supposedly is not involved with except for selling arms, have killed well over 600,000 civilians. At the moment there are over 70,000,000 people displaced by war around the world. Do you find these figures disturbing? Circle YES or NO...

Stalin is quoted as saying, "One person's death is a tragedy, but the death of a million people is a statistic." Do you think this is True or False?

Is there anything the common citizen can do about it? Do you have at least an idea:

____

____

The United States like many countries around the world has clamped down on immigration as if immigration is the root of all their problems.

After WW II do you think the United States should not have aided the devastated European countries but let them rebuild themselves? Circle your answer YES or NO...

After WW II should the United States have refused any European citizen the right to immigrate to the United States? Circle your answer YES or NO...

Did you know that after WWII many Jews were denied entrance to the United States? Circle YES or NO...

Did you know that before WWII a ship load of Jews was denied entrance to the United States and they were returned to Germany to be killed in extermination camps.

Do the above facts make you proud of your country? Circle YES or NO...and your reasoning:

____

____

If by some fluke of nature or a war the majority of the United States was decimated and millions of people were without food and shelter how many countries do you think would let Americans immigrate? Your answer:

____

____

Do you think Mexico would let us cross the Rio Grande River illegally and steal their low paying jobs? Circle YES or NO...

Vent sipped on his martini "Did you have a career?" Vent asked Julia.

"I was a nurse," Julia said, adding, "I found it very rewarding and although at times deeply sad it was also immensely uplifting."

"It takes a special person," Vent said in a way I knew he had a fondness for nurses. "I have been in the hospital several times and each time the treatment and care I received from nurses was overwhelming."

"I bet I was proposed to at least 50 times," Julia smiled

"There is a shortage of nurses now," I said.

"I know," Vent agreed. "It seems strange. It is a great job. It is a helping job. There are openings all over the country for nurses but they can never seem to fill all the slots."

"I don't understand it either," Julia said. "I try to get young people interested in a nursing career but few are willing."

Why do you think there is a nurse shortage when good jobs are difficult to find?

Circle your answer: THE PAY IS TOO LOW...PEOPLE ARE NOT INTELLIGENT ENOUGH TO PASS THE COURSES...TAKING CARE OF SICK PEOPLE IS NOT APPEALING.

It is not the pay. The average pay for a RN is $28.47 an hour or roughly $70,000 a year. If you live in a poor or rural area this is not true but the wage of a nurse in a poor area is far greater than the normal wage. With this kind of money why isn't the nursing field bursting with applications? Your reasoning:

____

____

Could it be the majority of people that are interested in nursing cannot afford the tuition and are afraid of carrying a staggering amount of debt? Circle your answer YES or NO...

After a few moments of silence I said, "People in the red states and conservatives are completely against socialism but they don't seem to realize how many socialist programs there are in the United States."

Vent finished his martini. He looked at Julia with imploring eyes but

Julia shook her head no.

"My father was an alcoholic," she said. "Two martinis are more than a sufficient amount to drink at one sitting."

"Let me define socialism and a few other political systems instead," Vent said accepting the fact he was not getting another martini. "Socialism originally was defined as a system in which goods and services are provided through a central system of cooperative, and or government ownership, rather than competition and a free market system. Marx and Lenin were socialists."

"A Democracy provides every legal citizen of a certain age with the free and equal right to participate in a system of government and elect representatives of the people by the majority of the people. When the person receiving the majority of the votes isn't the winner of an election then the country is not a democracy," Vent said. "For this reason, plus the fact you are not allowed to vote freely because of the practice of gerrymandering, the United States is not a democracy."

If you do not know what gerrymandering is look it up. You might be surprised how your voting rights are manipulated. But, at the moment, there are several cases before the Supreme Court attacking gerrymandering in several states that hopefully will lead to broad reform.

"When the Supreme Court ruled in favor of Citizens United the United States became a country where money replaced free speech and corporations have the same rights as people, we became an oligarchy. Today people have little control over the government while big corporations, wealthy donors, lobbyist, and Wall Street are free to influence elections," Vent said.

Is the United States an oligarchy? Circle YES or NO... and a space for your reasoning:

____

____

Does Wall Street and Big Business have more power over the government than you do as an average citizen? Circle YES or NO...

Why does the United States call itself a democracy when by definition and practice it is not? Your answer:

____

"The United States in many ways is headed in the direction of plutocracy. This form of government believes a society should be ruled by its wealthiest members. At the present time income equality is drowning and the middle class is disappearing, Republicans continue to block the minimum wage, and women do not receive equal pay for equal work," Vent said.

Is the United States becoming a plutocracy? Circle YES or NO...your reasoning:

"Many people in America are pushing for a theocracy where religious beliefs become the foundation for law," Vent added, "which is no different in principle than the Muslim nations. To make a point Congress recently established a dress code for women but did not set one for men."

Is the United States trying to become a theocracy? Circle YES or NO...your reasoning:

"A Republic is a form of government where the power resides with the people and the government is ruled by elected leaders who govern according to laws designed to help citizens," Vent said.

"Interesting," Julia said.

What do you think the United States is? Circle your answer: REPUBLIC...OLIGARCY...PLUTOCRACY...THEOCRACY...DEMOCRACY...and a space for your reasoning:

____

____

To get back to socialism, for all of you who are deathly against anything that could be construed as being socialist do you think the United States has any socialist programs? Circle YES or NO...if your answer was YES here is a space to list a few socialist programs:

____

____

If your answer was NO here are a few socialist programs for you to think about. There are many more if you wish to investigate further: Socialist programs include all branches of the military, Highway and Road Department, FEMA, Public Libraries, Police Departments, Fire Departments, Postal Service, Garbage Collection, CIA, FBI, Congressional Health Care, Museums, State and Federal Prisons not private, Corporate Business Subsidies, Public Parks, Court System, GI Bill, IRS, The Pentagon, Corporate Bailouts, Amtrak, The department of Homeland Security, Veterans Administration, Social Security, Medicare, SSI, Foster Care, Food Stamps, Unemployment Compensation, Child Care Food Program, Public Housing, Farm Aid, Pell Grants,

Public Education, Job Corps, Airport Controllers, Appalachian Regional Development, and any aid program given to states by the Federal Government. As I stated earlier there are many more socialist programs, 75 to be exact.

Since the United States has many socialist programs should they all be scraped so we can continue to try to convince many countries around the world we are a democracy? Circle YES or NO...your reasoning:

____

____

Merely for curiosities sake. Do you think Canadians want their country to be like the United States? Circle YES or NO...

Do you think Germans want Germany to be like the United States? Circle YES or NO...

Do you think the Swiss, the most evenly wealth managed country in the world, wishes to be like the United States? Circle YES or NO...

Have you ever heard of a person from Switzerland putting their money in an American bank? Circle your answer YES or NO...

Do Denmark, Finland, and Sweden want to be like the United States? Circle YES or NO..,

Does Saudi Arabia want to be like the United States? Circle YES or NO...

If you can think of any, list a few countries that would like to be like the United States.

____

If there are countries that want to be like the United States why are they not like the United States? Your answer:

Julia glanced at her watch. "I am going to leave you two alone," she said. "I hope to see you again Vent before you head back to Kansas City, but if I don't I wish you well and I hope many of the absurdities in our modern world get solved."

Vent stood and they hugged. "I am happy for you and William and I wish you the best. But when it comes to our world ever becoming rational I have my doubts."

I walked Julia to her car. "I think there is something physically wrong with Vent," Julia said sounding deeply concerned.

"He is not as animated as he was the first time we met but he seems fine," I answered.

"No, there is something wrong with him," she said again, kissed me goodbye on the cheek, got in her car, and drove away.

Julia's words did not set easy with me.

Vent had just finished making himself another martini. "When the cat is away and you know the rest of the saying," he said with a boyish grin.

"I'll take one," I replied.

Martinis in hand we sat at the kitchen table. "Julia seems to be extremely caring," Vent said.

"She has a huge heart. A heart so good she is always upbeat and can find good in almost anything."

"There are always a few people that seem to be able to stay upbeat and positive when everything seems to be depressing," Vent said.

"I have never had that ability," I admitted.

"Me either," Vent said.

"What do you think about the present day administration contemplating reducing the size of our National Monuments?" I asked.

"The powers that be have no foresight or vision. They only think in the present and the dependency on fossil fuels. What they are looking for is more land to mine, lumber to cut, and oil to drill. They do not seem to understand the future is in sustainable power like solar, wind, and tidal, and things yet to be discovered. All they see is immediate cash. Coal and gasoline are on their way out. It is only a matter of time before fossil fuels have to be replaced," Vent said.

Do you think that renewable energy sources are the wave of the future? Circle YES or NO...

Do you think more money should go into renewable energy than into fossil fuels? Circle YES or NO...

Do you see the coal industry rebounding? Circle your answer YES or NO...a space for your reasoning:

____

Is trying to revive the coal industry like trying to bring back the Model T? Circle YES or NO...

Since the end of World War II the demand for coal has steadily decreased. The main reason being many of its uses have been replaced by natural gas which is cheaper and also more environmentally friendly.

Do you think the need for gasoline will increase or decrease over the next fifty years? Circle your answer YES or NO...your reasoning:

Why is it the nations in Europe are more advanced than we are in the pursuit of solar and wind power? Circle your answer: THEY ARE SMARTER THAN WE ARE...THEY ARE DUMBER THAN WE ARE BECAUSE GAS AND COAL WILL LAST FOREVER...AMERICANS HAVE LIVED SO LONG ON THEIR LAURELS THEY HAVE BECOME STUPID...a space if you have another answer:

"Recently there has been a tremendous amount of name calling by proponents of one political persuasion against those of another political persuasion," Vent said. "I have a series of questions for you that I believe most people could not truthfully or knowingly answer."

Here are Vent's questions with the answers following. No alternative facts I promise.

What is a Liberal? Your answer:

____

____

Answer: Liberals believe in government action to achieve equal opportunity and equality for all. It is the duty of the government to alleviate social ills and to protect civil liberties and individual and human rights. Liberals believe the role of the government should be to guarantee that no one is in need. Liberal policies generally emphasize the need for the government to solve problems. Democrats at the present time are considered liberals.

What is a conservative? Your answer:

____

____

Answer: Conservatives believe in personal responsibility, limited government, free markets, individual liberty, traditional American values and a strong national defense. They believe the role of the government should be to provide people the freedom necessary to pursue their own goals. Republicans are considered conservatives.

To confuse the issue there are many factions of liberals and there are many factions of conservatives that are constantly bickering among themselves.

Here is a partial list on what Liberals and Conservatives differ over:

Abortion, Affirmative Action, The Death Penalty, Economy, Education (public vs. charter), Stem Cell Research, Energy, Physician Assisted Suicide, Global Warming and Climate Change, Gun Control, Healthcare, Planned Parenthood, Homeland Security, Immigration, Private Property, Religion and Government, Same Sex Marriage, Social Security, Taxes, The United Nations, War On Terror, and Welfare. And a space for you to add anything else you can think of:

____

____

Here is a list on what Liberals and Conservatives agree on: 0....They agree on nothing.

Maybe this is why the country is the way it is...divided. Do you think that Liberals and Conservatives should learn how to compromise? Circle YES or NO...and your reasoning:

____

____

Does anyone ever get everything they ask for? Circle YES or NO...

The answer is NO.

Vent and I finished our martinis at the same time. “It is really nice to see you

William,” Vent said. “We only met for a few short hours in Kansas City but after you left it seemed as though I had known you for my entire life.”

"Maybe before we were alive we were spirits and we knew each other," I said.

"Sounds good but I doubt it," Vent said.

Do you think there is a chance, no matter how minuscule, that before we become flesh we are a spirit? Circle YES or NO...

The Mormons believe when a person is born a soul comes down from heaven and joins their body? Is this hard to believe? Circle YES or NO...

"Do you think it strange that Moses lost God's Ten Commandments that were etched on stone and Joseph Smith somehow misplaced God's commandments that were etched on solid gold? Circle YES or NO...

If you had several bars of gold would you misplace them? Circle YES or NO...

Where do angels come from? Your answer:

____

____

Is it feasible that there was a God that created the modern God? Circle YES or NO and a space for your answer:

____

____

If there was a God that created the modern God will the modern God create the God that will exist one million years from now? Circle YES or NO and a space for your reasoning:

Throughout time each different group of people or nation has had their own God or Gods. When a nation and their God or Gods are defeated in war by another nation and their God or Gods, what happens to the defeated GOD or Gods? Circle your answer: THEY GO TO A RETIRMENT HOME FOR DISCARDED GODS...THEY GO TO THE FAR CORNERS OF SPACE AND SULK...THEY BLAME PEOPLE FOR THEIR LOUSY LOT AND BECOME ALCOHOLICS AND DRUG ADDICTS...you answer if you don't think any of the above are correct.

What will happen to God when humanity has finally destroyed itself? Circle your answer: GOD WILL REDOCORATE THE KIDS ROOM...GOD WILL HAVE A PARTY...GOD WILL HOPE THERE IS NO SUCH THING AS REINCARNATION... GOD WILL LEARN FROM HIS MISTAKES AND NEVER MAKE BEINGS IN HIS IMAGE AGAIN...or your ideas:

If there was no mankind would God still exist? Circle YES or NO...no matter your answer please explain your reasoning:

____

____

"Why did you come to Phoenix?" I blurted out unable to control my curiosity any longer.

"I came to visit you and an old army friend," Vent answered. "He is not doing well and I wanted to see him one more time."

There was something in Vent's voice that I knew without a doubt he was telling me an alternative truth.

"I think I mentioned this before but I never kept in touch with any of the guys I served with in Vietnam," I said. "In 1967 I wanted to forget everything. There are times I wonder how their lives turned out. But I could walk by any of them now and probably would not recognize them."

"There is a difference in serving in a war that is considered a good war and one that is not," Vent said.

I nodded. What was there to say? Nothing can be done to change the past – either the realities or the attitudes.

Can anything be done to change the past? Circle YES or NO...

If your answer was NO why do we waste so much time looking back?

____

"Would you take me to my hotel?" Vent asked. "It has been a long day and I am tired."

Vent was staying at the Renaissance Hotel off of Hwy 101. Tt would not take long to get there.

"At night all big cities look the same," Vent said as we drove. "The cars on the freeway are merely a nuisance and the brightly lit buildings are giant Christmas trees that never dry up and get tossed in the dump. It makes me feel slightly in awe but also slightly revolted at the grandeur and waste of it all."

"After the war I wanted to own a cabin in the mountains," I said. "I wanted to distance myself from the world. I wanted a simple life. Chop wood to heat and cook, grow a garden, hunt and fish. I did it for several years and I discovered much to my dismay the devastation of forest fires and storms, insects eat gardens, and animals and fish just don't jump into the frying pan. It was both a good and sobering experience but now I like the convenience of the big city."

"More and more people are moving back to the city," Vent said.

"I think life is nothing but a succession of being ironic," I mused.

Has your life been a succession of being ironic? Circle YES or NO...

If it has not been ironic what has it been? A space for your answer:

"I'll call you tomorrow afternoon," Vent informed me as I stopped in front of the hotel.

Walking away there was a slight stoop to Vent's shoulders and no trace of rebellion in his steps. I felt sad with the realization Vent was completely alone in the world. I had the urge to get out of the car, put my arm on his shoulder, and say, "Vent, it will be ok," but I did not. For many things in life this is how it is - we feel a need radiating from a person and we do nothing.

Question? Why is it we do not help our fellow human beings more often? Circle your answer: WE DON'T CARE... WE FEEL IT WILL DO NO GOOD... WE ARE TOO BUSY...and space for reasons you might have that I did not mention:

____

____

The next morning I was jittery with anticipation over having to wait to see Vent. I cleaned the apartment. I took the car to a car wash and washed and vacuumed it. By 3 pm I was glancing at the clock every few minutes wondering when Vent would call. Julia called at 3:15 saying she thought it best that I enjoy my visit with Vent and after he headed back to Kansas City to call. She was right, but, it still made me slightly guilty that I would rather see Vent without her. Relationships are funny things. Do you ever feel guilty when you are doing something you really like to do by yourself when you think about your significant other? Circle YES or NO...whatever your answer was here is a space to explain why:

____

____

After Julia's call I went over and over in my mind anything that would indicate Vent was not feeling well. The only thing I thought was he did not twitch or get excited when we discussed topics. I decided Julia must be wrong. Vent was not ill. It was only in her nurse's mind.

When the phone rang at 4:00 pm I picked it up like it was news I had won the lottery. "I am glad you are still alive," Vent said.

"Me too," I replied. "I find that being alive each day is a great benefit to the act of living."

"Why don't you pick me up in an hour? I will wait for you out front and we can go to supper," Vent said.

I cringed. In an hour I would be driving in rush hour traffic. Driving in rush hour traffic is like having to face your worst fears at the same time everyday. It is a reoccurring nightmare. In Arizona there is also the fear you will get shot and killed by some road rage zombie with NRA stickers all over their truck who is in a hurry to get to the anti-immigration rally where the speaker, unknowing to the audience, is starting a company teaching white people how to pick fruit and vegetables, live in shacks, and survive on minimum wage and no healthcare.

I remember Phoenix years ago when there were no super highways and you drove right through the middle of town to get to L.A. hoping you would not hit every stoplight. It now takes close to an hour to drive through town on the interstate and that is if you plan your trip at about two in the morning. This problem will be eradicated when the water finally runs out in Arizona and all the dessert rats scurry to Washington or Oregon and learn how to complain about the rain and slugs in their flower beds and gardens.

Question? Are there any states where it is illegal to catch rain water for use on your own private property? Circle YES or NO...

Strangely the answer is YES.

In how many states is it illegal to capture rain water? Circle your answer: TWO...FOUR...SIX...EIGHT...NINE...FIFTEEN...TWENTY...THRITY...

The answer is EIGHT: There used to be nine but Colorado recently had a change of heart and discarded their law against rain barrels. The states where it is illegal are Oregon, Ohio, California, Nevada, Texas, Utah, Illinois, and Idaho. I take it the government figures the rain falling from the sky over their state belongs to them and since there are not enough things illegal and regulated by the state they might as well make having a rain barrel illegal. They can then appropriate money for Rain Barrel Cops by cutting the education budget. I have heard, in the states defense, that rain barrels cause higher crime rates, people with rain barrels have a tendency to grow gardens and therefore hurt the grocery store conglomerates, and rain barrels may start children on the path of water pipes. There is also a conspiracy rumor going around that rain barrels are trying to take over the world and are plotting an all out war on sprinklers.

Do you think that making rain collection illegal is going a little too far? Circle

YES or NO...your reasoning:

____

____

I do find it ironic that Oregon and Nevada have made catching rain on your own property illegal but you can buy marijuana and all its by-products. I wonder if some enterprising individual is working on a way to manufacture rain barrels from marijuana stalks.

Do you believe that when a product is illegal it raise people's interest in it?

Circle YES or NO...

More people drank alcohol during prohibition than after and in states where marijuana has been made legal marijuana use has gone down by citizens of the state – a huge part of the market is from out of state people.

Vent, looking dapper in a light colored summer suit was waiting for me.

"Too bad the weather is not like this all year," he said as he fastened his seatbelt. "I think the 110 to 120 degree days in the summer would do me in."

"The summer does a lot of people in," I said. "The murder rate triples."

Is oppressive temperature a good reason to kill someone? Circle YES or NO...

"I know we had enchiladas last night but is there a Mexican restaurant you like close by?" Vent asked which is a polite way of saying, "I'd like Mexican food," without asking me if I wanted to eat Mexican food again.

Here is an off-the-wall question. Do you think Mexicans ever get tired of eating Mexican food? Circle YES or NO...

Do Italians ever get tired of eating pasta? Circle YES or NO...

I never get tired of eating Chinese food.

Is the ability to eat the food one wishes being spoiled? Circle YES or NO...

"There are about 50,000 Mexican restaurants in town," I said, but my favorite is Lucy's."

"I bet you can get Mexican food in any country in the world," Vent said.

Do you think there is a Mexican restaurant in Iraq? Circle YES or NO...

How about any Middle Eastern country? Circle YES or NO...

Are there Mexican restaurants in China? Circle YES or NO...

How many Chinese restaurants do you think there are in the United States? Circle your answer: 10,000, 15,000, 25,000, 50,000, 100,000...and a blank if you think none of the above are correct:

____

According to Chinese Restaurant News there are 41,000 Chinese restaurants in the United States generating over 17 billion dollars in yearly sales. There are three times the number of Chinese Restaurants than McDonalds franchise units, which leads to this question. Is Chinese food better for you than McDonalds? Circle your answer YES or NO...

Lucy's Mexican Restaurant has been in business for thirty years. It reminds me of a cafe in a Mexican border town where tourists would be afraid to eat. It is not a place for the picky eater as they cook their taco shells in lard and there is also lard in the refried beans. To quote a waitress, "We don't use no stinking vegetable or granola oil here. This is real Mexican food made by real Mexicans."

Is there such a think as an unreal Mexican? YES or NO...

How about an unreal white person? YES or NO...

How about an unreal human being? Circle YES or NO...

Their green and red salsa is extremely hot and only for the brave. When you start coughing and fanning your mouth the workers and other patrons will laugh and point at you like your suffering is the funniest thing they have seen in years.

Vent and I each ordered a south of the border beer from a jovial middle aged Hispanic lady wearing jeans, pink shoes, and a black T-shirt that stated in blood red letters TRUMP SUCKS AND IF YOU WANT MY JOB WHITE PEOPLE YOU CAN HAVE IT. I will not tell you the name of the beer because before I started this book I contacted the beer company and offered to mention their beer for what I considered a nominal fee. They refused stating my book would not sell enough copies to be worth the advertising, which is probably true, but it still hurt my feelings. None-the-less I like the beer.

"Do you know that Mexican beer is cheaper in Hawaii than on the mainland," Vent said.

"How can that be?" I asked.

"I have no idea but I know NAFTA has nothing to do with it," Vent replied.

Here is a space for you to explain how Mexican beer can be cheaper in Hawaii than on the mainland:

____

____

Since Trump's stand on NFTA has been in the news constantly here is a space for you to explain what NFTA is:

____

____

If you do not know look it up. I will inform you that Trump is always stating we work on a trade imbalance. Sorry, fake news, the reason there is a trade imbalance is because we import more than we export. Call up Trump and ask him to start mixing in a few truths with his lies.

On the other hand do you think it is possible for Trump to tell the truth? Circle YES or NO...

Do you want your taxes to pay for the wall along the border with Mexico even though Trump stated Mexico would pay for the wall? Circle YES or NO...

Can you really trust someone with a sprayed on tan? Circle YES or NO...

“Did you see your old army friend today?” I asked Vent.

Vent hesitated like he did not want to answer my question, finally replying in a way that reminded me of a little boy telling a white lie, “He is in bad shape. The doctors informed him he only has a few weeks to live.”

“I am sorry but at least you were able to see him,” I said.

“We will say our goodbyes tomorrow,” Vent said but he didn’t seem overly sad.

“I have said goodbye to several dieing friends,” I said. “It always seems surreal and awkward.”

“Saying goodbye to someone on their deathbed or going to a funeral is just practicing for our own death,” Vent said.

Do you think we practice for our own death? Circle YES or NO...

Do you think thinking about death is morbid? Circle YES or NO...

Do you want to die? Circle YES or NO...

Would you like to know when you were going to die? Circle YES or NO...

The waitress brought the beers, a bowl of green salsa and a bowl of red salsa, a basket of warm tortilla chips, and menus. Why she didn’t bring the menus when we first came in I have no idea but I suppose we all have our own weird way of doing things. Before I could tell Vent to be careful with the salsa he dipped a huge pile of both red and green salsa on a chip and tossed it in his mouth. I waited for the outcry. The waitress waited for the outcry. Vent chewed, swallowed, filled another chip and tossed it in his mouth. Chewed, swallowed, drank some beer, and said, “Good salsa, great flavor, hot, but not so hot it takes your head off.”

“You should have been a Mexican,” the waitress said with admiration.

I put a small amount of each salsa on a chip thinking maybe it was a mild batch. It was hot as hell but there was no way I was going to let on I didn’t think it was any more than spicy.

Several tables away four women were merrily snapping pictures of their food and posting them on one or all of the 3,478 social websites. “What do you think about people taking pictures of what they are eating?” I asked Vent.

Vent couldn’t answer right away as he was chopping down on another salsa laden chip. “Pictures of food have never greatly excited me,” he said.

If I sent you a picture of what I was eating would you get greatly excited? Circle YES or NO...

Do you really care what other people are eating? Circle YES or NO...

Do you think people who post pictures of the food they are eating in restaurants are in all truth self centered jerks trying to rub it in your face that while they are able to eat out you are at home cooking like a peasant? Circle YES or NO...

If you answered NO here is a space for your reasoning:

____

____

The waitress returned, noticed we had not picked up the menus and without asking said, “I’ll bring you gentlemen two more beers.”

“Now that is a real waitress,” Vent complimented.

When the beers were delivered we ordered. Vent ordered the green chile stew and I ordered the combination plate.

After taking a bite of the stew Vent asked, “Do you think the Chicago Cubs will ever win a World Series again?”

“I don’t think it really matters now. The big draw was them winning one,” I said.

Do you think that since the Chicago Cubs won the World Series there are as many people rooting for them? Circle YES or NO...

Do you think if the Cubs and the Cleveland Indians played again in a World Series more people would root for Cleveland? Circle YES or NO...

Why is it that the majority of mankind will root for the underdog? Your answer:

____

____

Even if baseball is the American game I think it is boring. Do you think baseball is boring? Circle YES or NO...

If you answered YES what can be done to pep the game up at least a notch or two?

____

____

“Vent, in your lifetime have you ever seen the country as divided as it is now?” I asked.

“There has always been division,” Vent said, “but I don’t think we have ever been this divided since the Civil War.”

“What can be done about it?” I asked.

With a wry smile Vent replied, “Nothing. It will follow the course it is going to follow.”

Do you think anything can be done to stop the division in the United States?

Circle YES or NO...a space for your reasoning:

____

____

If senators and congressmen are really concerned about the country why can’t they figure something out to stop the division? Circle your answer: THEY ARE ONLY CONCERNED ABOUT THEMSELVES...THEY ARE IDIOTS...ALL OF THE ABOVE...

Maybe the leaders we have elected are nothing but spoiled brats who we have allotted too much power over us. Do you think the American public has become too complacent concerning our politicians? Circle YES or NO...

What can be done about it?

____

____

Vent finished his bowl of green chili. “That was superb,” he said.

“Is the coffee shop we went to in Kansas City still open,” I asked.

“They had to close, rent downtown has become prohibitive,” Vent answered.

“That is too bad,” I said.

“The good old capitalist system,” Vent replied wryly.

“Maybe it is time to move to the mountains and live off the grid?” I said.

“Florida and Texas have made it illegal to live off the grid,” Vent said.

Do you think this is fake news? Circle YES or NO...

In fact it is not fake news. In Florida and Texas you have to hook up to the grid, which means you would have to at a minimum pay a meter fee. If you are thinking about living off the grid you had better check your state and local laws.

In the majority of states if you own land without a house on it and stay on the land in a tent or camper for more than two weeks you need to get a camping permit. If you were camping on your own land would you get a permit? Circle YES or NO...

There are also many municipalities that do not allow tiny homes because they do not meet the square foot requirement. Do you think in the land of the free and the home of the brave you should be able to live on your own property the way you wish and build a home the size you wish? Circle YES or NO...

In many states as of the writing of this book electric companies are trying to have laws passed that people with solar panels have to pay a higher rate for the electricity they use from the grid. Is this right? Circle YES or NO...

Is there anything you can think of that big business, with the government’s blessing, hasn’t been able to regulate? A space if you can think of anything?

____

____

A fact: Of the few tariffs Trump has imposed one is against solar panels. The number one growing industry in the United States is the solar industry. Did oil and gas lobbying groups have anything to do with this. Circle YES or NO...

I noticed Vent seemed distracted. There were things going on in his head that had nothing to do with what we were talking about.

“Are you tired,” I asked.

“I feel tired but I also feel let down and discouraged,” Vent said. “I thought that during my lifetime there would be huge strides towards world peace. There would be an end to prejudice. There would be a universal awakening that if we didn’t get our acts together many dire things would happen. But nothing has really changed. It seems as though every stride forward for the good of mankind is followed by two steps backward.”

Do you think life is always taking one step forward and then two steps backward? Circle YES or NO...

Or do you think that mankind is doing exactly what it was intended to do? Circle YES or NO...

Was mankind intended to: Circle your answers: OVER POPULATE THE WORLD, HAVE WARS OVER RELIGION, BELIEVE THEIR RACE IS BETTER THAN ANOTHER RACE, THINK THEY HAVE DOMINION OVER ALL CREATURES ON THE FACE OF THE EARTH,

POLLUTE THE WORLD...a space if you wish to add a few more:

____

____

Here is room for you to list what you think mankind was intended to do:

____

____

"There are many people and organizations that try their best to help and better mankind," I said to try and cheer Vent up.

"That's true," Vent agreed. "They are of a much higher moral fiber than I am as they take physical action while I only protest with words."

"You could be like President Carter and build houses or you could join the Peace Corp," I said.

"I started volunteering at a soup kitchen in Kansas City," Vent said. "It is a sobering experience."

"Homelessness is a condition that should not exist in this country," I added.

"There are many things that burden my mind," Vent said.

Is there any time when life is not a burden? Circle YES or NO...

What do you do to improve your mental state when things start to wear you down? List your remedies:

"Let's go to the hotel bar," Vent suggested while waving for the check.

Vent paid the bill leaving a more than generous tip.

The one thing I like about hotel bars, even though they are normally overpriced, is the fact the background music is seldom so loud you have to scream at each other to be heard. Vent and I sat at a corner table. I always feel like a gangster sitting at a corner table but it is also the best table for people watching. If you are not into people watching you can sit with your face facing the wall. If you do sit facing the wall it is for sure you are not a gangster.

True to form Vent ordered a vodka martini. I ordered a gin and tonic. "Hotels have always intrigued me ever since I was a young boy," Vent said. "They are like a small city composed of people from all over the country for one brief night. I have met many different people and had many informative conversations talking to strangers in a hotel bar."

"Most of the hotels I have stayed at I was afraid I would get bed bugs and the bar was some dive on the corner," I joked.

Vent chuckled but I could tell he was not really amused.

Do you ever laugh at a bad joke only because you do not want to hurt the teller's feelings? Circle YES or NO...

"Do you think ISIS will ever be truly defeated?" I asked.

"Believing Middle Eastern terrorism will be crushed is like thinking a can of raid will wipe out all the mosquitoes in Louisiana," Vent said. "We might defeat their armies but it will not stop individual terrorist attacks against civilians. Terrorists are recruited from poor countries where there is very little hope of changing one's life. As long as there is hunger and poverty in the Middle East there will be people and organizations that are willing to kill and die for their beliefs."

Do you think that the same holds true in the United States for people born and raised in the slums? Circle YES or NO...your reasoning:

____

____

If you were born in a slum would you feel cheated by society? Circle YES or NO...

If you were born in a slum what would you do to try and get out of the slum?

____

____

If you were born in a slum and failed in all your attempts to get out of the slum would you join a gang? Circle YES or NO...

If you would not join a gang what would you do? Your answer:

____

Have you ever heard of a rich man robbing corner convenience stores just for the rush? Circle YES or NO...

"The president has sworn to wipe out gangs," Vent said. "Maybe he should try to wipe out poverty."

If there was less poverty would there be fewer gangs? Circle YES or NO.

If a person who committed a large white collar crime was put to death would it in any way hinder others from engaging in white collar crime? Circle YES or NO...

People say that the death penalty deters crime. Do you think this is true? Circle YES or NO...

If it is true why does the United States have more incarcerated people than any other country in the world? A space for your answer:

"In 1967 I had a job working for a newspaper in Newark, NJ," I said. "I had never been exposed to such massive poverty or cops that obviously singled out black people. I witnessed cops beating people for no reason, taking kick backs on drug deals, and guarding whore houses. I lived in a small apartment above a family of gypsies. The father made his living stealing and stripping cars. The wife read palms and the kids were pickpockets. The day the Newark riot erupted I rode around town on the back of a motorcycle while a black friend of mine drove. The only thing I never understood about the riot was why didn't the rioters burn the white side of town instead of their own?"

"Anger, once unleashed, has no common sense," Vent said. "All the frustration boils over into an uncontrollable rage."

"Needless to say when the riot was over I moved away from the East Coast," I said.

"Ferguson, Missouri was no different," Vent said. "White cops in the majority of a police force in a primarily black community can only lead to problems."

"I always wondered why bad cops don't get assassinated," I said. "The community knows which ones are bad."

"I have wondered that myself," Vent replied.

Have you ever wondered why bad cops just don't disappear one day and are never seen again. If a cop killed your unarmed son or daughter would you want to kill him? Circle YES or NO...

Do you think you could kill a bad cop and get away with it? Circle YES or NO...

Do you think the unfair treatment the police have been guilty of for many years against minorities has lead to violence against the police? Circle YES or NO...

If you answered NO what has lead to violence against the police?

____

____

Our drinks were delivered. We held our drinks up in a toast. "To love and understanding," Vent said.

“Both are difficult,” I said.

“Julia loves you. It is obvious,” Vent said.

“How do you know?” I asked. Inwardly knowing it was true.

“The way she smiles at you. How she listens to you when you talk.”

“I miss her when she is gone,” I said.

“Do you love her?” Vent asked.

“I know I enjoy her company. I know I am comfortable around her. I know I can tell her what I feel even though she might not feel the same way, but I don’t know if I can truly say I know what love is even though I feel I love her.”

Does not understanding what love is but knowing you are in love make any sense to you? Circle YES or NO...

“Maybe love is something we really shouldn’t try to define,” Vent said. “Maybe love is comfort, or friendship. I don’t think anyone really knows what love is. I think love is unique to each person.”

Do you think love is something that should not be defined? Circle YES or NO...

Here is a space if you think you can define love:

____

____

“I do know I am not 18 year old head over heals I can not live without you in love,” I said.

“It would have been nice to have been in love at 18, married, and still be with the same person when you are old," Vent said.

What is the divorce rate in America? Circle your answer: 20%...25%...30%... 35%... 40%...50%...60%...

The answer is between 40% and 50% of people who get married will get a divorce.

Do rich or poor people divorce more often? Circle your answer RICH or POOR...

The answer is POOR.

On the average do first marriages last longer than second or third marriages? Circle your answer: FIRST...SECOND...THIRD...after three marriages who cares...

The answer is first marriages last longer.

For information sake Nevada, Maine, Oklahoma, Florida, Oregon and Kentucky have the highest rate of divorce.

New York, New Jersey, Utah, California, and North Dakota have the lowest rate of divorce.

Do you have any idea why some states have higher divorce rates than others?

Circle YES or NO...

If you answered NO do not fret the majority of so called marriage councilors do not know either.

What is the percentage of married people who have an affaire? Circle your answer: 10%...20%...30%...40%...50%...60%...70%...

The rate of infidelity is 60%.

Do men cheat more than women? Circle your answer MEN...WOMEN...

It used to be men, but now men and women are equal when it comes to infidelity. The main reason is women are now an integral part of the work force and spend more time at their work than at home – thus more time to stray.

“You should tell Julia you love her,” Vent said.

“It think she knows,” I said. “But you are right I should tell her.”

I signaled for another round of drinks. The bar was filling up with men wearing suits with their ties loosened. For some strange reason I have always wondered what fashion quirk made it that businessmen wear suits and ties. In time people will look back at what we now wear and wonder what in the hell were they thinking. It will be like modern people looking at paintings of 16th and 17th century European kings and queens. The peasants at the time wore rags like our modern peasants so with them there is really no great difference.

“How many more years are you going to sell cars? Vent asked as our drinks were delivered.

“I have a decent nest egg and will draw full Social Security soon,” I said. “I have been thinking about buying a Class C motor home and asking Julia if she would like to drive around the country for at least a year. There are so many places I would like to see. The only thing that scares me is the cost of an RV and I what would happen if I happened to get sick”

“Hopefully the government won’t borrow from the Social Security fund and not pay it back like they have before,” Vent said.

Why does the government always call Social Security an entitlement when it is not an entitlement at all? Circle your answer: THEY ARE LIARS...THEY THINK THE MAJORITY OF AMERICANS ARE STUPID...

Also, why do news broadcasters also call Social Security an entitlement when they know it is not? Circle your answer: THE NEWS AGENCIES SECRETLY WORK FOR THE GOVERNMENT...THEY ARE STUPID...

“I do know that Social Security has nothing to do with the national deficit,” I said.

“It is a self sustaining program run on people’s money and the businesses they work for.”

“Wall Street wants to see Social Security privatized,” Vent said. “To date they have invested more than 1 billion dollars to various lobbying groups to push for repeal of Social Security.”

“Seems to me they should be worried about the country’s debt,” I said.

“Over 1/3rd of the government’s debt is owned by foreign countries with China being the largest owner of the United States debt. Russia owns a huge chunk of our debt and the United States government owes the Federal Reserve over five trillion.

Do you like the idea of the government being in debt to China? Circle YES or NO...

Did you know that China has purchased huge amounts of United States government bonds? Circle YES or NO...

If we are in debt to China, and they own a huge amount of our bonds, how can the United States make trade deals that would benefit the American people without making concessions? A space for your answer:

____

____

Do you think it is strange that we owe money to Russia? Circle YES or NO...

Would you loan money to the government? Circle YES or NO...

If you did loan money to the government would you want a few favors in return? Circle YES or NO...

Did you know that the bank of Brazil is a huge world bank? Circle YES or NO...

Did you know that the United States owes huge sums of money to the Bank of Brazil? Circle YES or NO...

“Do you think many aspects of what the government does now should be privatized,” I asked Vent.

“If the Highway Department was privatized most roads would be toll roads,” Vent said.

Would you like the majority of roads to be toll roads? Circle YES or NO...

If public schools were privatized you would have to pay to send your children to school. Would you like this? Circle YES or NO...

Bridges built and maintained by private business would become toll bridges.

The drinks were delivered. “The martinis they make here are not as good as the ones Julia makes,” Vent said.

“The best martini I ever drank was at a small bar in downtown Chicago close to the train station. The bartender used one part Absolute vodka, one part Bombay Sapphire gin, two drops of Vermouth, one drop of olive juice, and two olives. He said a martini could have one olive or two but never three. I was in town on business and spent three evenings there. Several years later I was back in Chicago but the bar had closed. I have tried many times to make the same martini but I don’t have the magic touch,” I said.

“When I was a bartender I could never get the right amount of ice crystals in my martinis or cosmopolitans,” Vent said.

“I would be a good bartender in a bar that only served beer,” I stated truthfully.

“What are your feelings about the allegations Trump and Russia worked together during the elections?” Vent asked.

"Trump saying he never did business with Russia or tried to do business with Russia has to be an alternate truth but since he is already our fearless lying leader what difference does it make if he was in cahoots with Russia or not?" I answered.

"None," Vent said. "If Trump would be impeached then we would be stuck with Pence, who, in my opinion, would be worse. Then we would have to listen to a sermon every day and a person who does not believe in climate change."

Do you care if Trump cut deals with Russia? Circle YES or NO...a space for your reasoning either way:

____

____

Do you care if Russia helped Trump become president? Circle YES or NO...your reasoning either way:

____

____

Do you feel like a pawn? Circle YES or NO...

If you do not feel like a pawn what do you feel like? Circle your answer: CONFUSED...USED...HELPLESS...A TRUE RED WHITE AND BLUE AMERICAN...a space if none of these state how you feel:

____

____

"Have you ever thought about artificial intelligence?" Vent asked.

"Stephen Hawking believes artificial intelligence could be the end of mankind," I replied.

"He also believes it is almost too late for mankind to turn around our caustic environmental behavior and we will eventually destroy ourselves," Vent said.

"If mankind does not destroy itself will there come a time when we develop artificial intelligence to the extent it can be placed in robots. These robots, possessing all of our knowledge, will then be able to expand their own knowledge, and in time will be able to replicate themselves without our help. When this happens there will be no need for our life form," I said.

Do you think in time robots will be able to replicate themselves? Circle YES or NO...

Could robots in time, with their superior knowledge, grow tired of our stupidity and make mankind their slaves? Circle YES or NO...

If you answered YES does the idea scare you? Circle YES or NO...

Will the development of robots for business purposes continue? Circle YES or No...

If you answered YES will the development of robots for business cause more unemployment? Circle YES or NO...

If your answer was NO where will the people that are displaced by robots work?

A space for your answer:

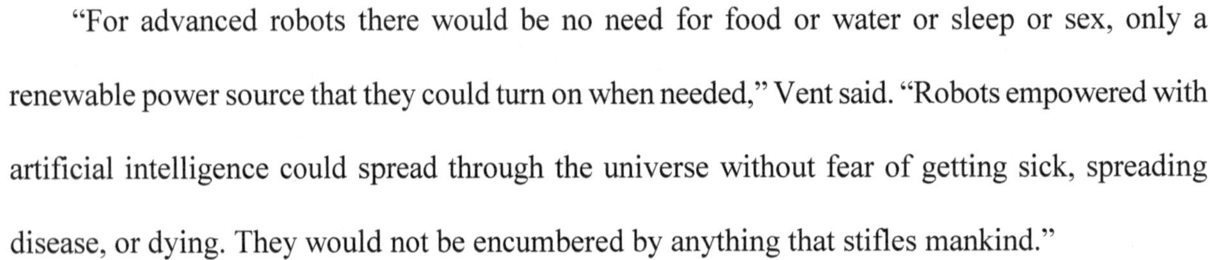

"For advanced robots there would be no need for food or water or sleep or sex, only a renewable power source that they could turn on when needed," Vent said. "Robots empowered with artificial intelligence could spread through the universe without fear of getting sick, spreading disease, or dying. They would not be encumbered by anything that stifles mankind."

"There would be no need for God," I said.

"There is no reason to think artificial intelligence would not see a need for a God," Vent said.

Do you think artificial intelligence would think there was a need for a God? Circle YES or NO...and your reasoning:

____

____

"Maybe robots would consider mankind their God since we created them," Vent said.

"Would artificial intelligence shun greed or war or class distinction?" I asked.

"True intelligence cannot embrace these things," Vent said.

"Some people think we are the first experiment in artificial intelligence," I said.

Do you think we are an experiment in artificial intelligence? Circle YES or NO...

If you answered YES do you think we are an experiment that did not turn out the way it was planned? Circle YES or NO...

If an explorative group of robots with artificial intelligence landed on earth what would they think about mankind?

Circle your answer? PRIMITIVE...STUPID... INTELLIGENT...IGNORANT...TO BE AVOIDED...CRUEL...LOVING...a space to explain your answer:

____

____

If an explorative group of robots with artificial intelligence landed on earth and observed what we have done to the planet what would they think? Circle your answer: WE HAVE NO FORSIGHT...WE HAVE BEEN GOOD STEWARDS OF OUR PLANET...WE ARE TERRIBLE STEWARDS OF OUR PLANET...your opinion:

____

____

“I don’t want another drink,” Vent said after finishing his martini.

“Would you like a cup of coffee? I asked.

“Decaf would be nice,” he said, which surprised me. In Kansas City when we drank coffee he started with a triple shot of espresso, went to a double, and finished it off with a single.

We both ordered a decaf coffee.

“If I drink regular coffee in the evening I might not sleep for days,” Vent said. “It is really too bad as I used to really enjoy coffee after dinner, the stronger the better."

"Decaf coffee is like drinking non-alcoholic beer," I said with a small amount of distain. "It is a trick we play on ourselves."

"When you think about it it is rather absurd," Vent agreed.

Is decaf coffee and non-alcoholic beer rather absurd? Circle your answer YES or NO...

Absurd or not they have made millions of dollars.

While I am on the topic of absurd I was in Portland, Oregon several months ago and there was a sign on a marijuana shop – GLUTEN FREE MARIJUANA. I had no idea marijuana had wheat in it or are pot heads that stupid? Or are some pot shops cutting their weed with wheat?

Two men started laughing at the bar and Vent glanced over at them. For some reason everything in the room except Vent's face disappeared from my vision. I noticed in glaring detail the weariness in his eyes. The anger and frustration at the atrocities in life that had been etched in the lines on his face when we first met were now a sad acceptance. Vent looked away from the men and our eyes locked for brief moment. In that moment we both knew, even though we had only known each other for a short time, we were closer than any other friends we had ever known.

The coffee was delivered. "Life is a journey that no one in the past or no one in the future will ever be able to understand," Vent said.

"There are a few times in my life when I felt the world had a predictable direction but they did not last," I said. "We are born in confusion, we live in confusion, and we die in confusion."

Do you believe life is normally confusing? Circle YES or NO...

If you answered YES does it have to be so confusing? Circle YES or NO...

We picked up our coffee cups and clicked them together in a toast to confusion.

“Do you think healthcare is a right of mankind,” I asked Vent.

“If you believe in Christian beliefs it is. If you believe only in the rules of capitalism it is not,” Vent said.

“Do you believe healthcare should be taken care of by the government? Circle your answer YES or NO...and a space for your opinion:

____

____

Do you really care if poor people have health insurance: Circle your answer YES or NO... and a blank for your reasoning:

____

____

Do you care if poor children eat? Circle your answer YES or NO...

Are rich people superior to poor people? Circle your answer YES or NO... your reasoning:

____

____

Do you think that the whole idea of health insurance is a joke and all health insurance should be eliminated – instead it would be a free market enterprise like gas stations or grocery stores or any other business? Each medical procedure would have a fee and if you could afford it you could go to the doctor, and if you couldn't you could stay sick and die. Circle your answer YES or NO...and your reasoning:

____

____

It is proven that rich people live longer than poor people.

Merely for your information here are the average costs for a few common medical procedures in the United States - procedure costs vary from area to area.

Hysterectomy - $15,400

Cornea operation per eye - $17,500

Gastric Bypass - $25,000

Knee replacement - $35,000

Angioplasty - $28,200

Hip replacement – $40,500

Heart Bypass - $123,000

Heart Valve Replacement - $170,000

Average Cost of Cancer treatment - $10,000 a month to $30,000 a month

Lung Transplant - $797,000

Liver Transplant - $575,000

Kidney Transplant - $262,000

Heart Transplant - $1,000,000

With the prices stated above how many of you could afford a medical procedure without insurance? Circle I COULD or I COULDN'T...

The cost for medical procedures in the United States runs anywhere from 25% to 75% higher than in Europe. Drug prices in the United States run on the average 60% higher than in Europe. The United States recently made it illegal for Americans to buy prescription drugs in Canada stating there was no proof Canadian drugs were safe although they are made buy the same companies that sell medicines in the United States. The majority of voters to turn down the legislation were Republicans although there were 13 Democrats that also voted no. Medications in Canada are on the average 65% cheaper than in the United States.

Is it wrong that United States citizens cannot buy medications in Canada? Circle YES or NO...your reasoning:

____

____

Do you think the pharmaceutical industry has any control over our congressmen? Circle YES or NO...

Why is it that the United States has the highest medical and drug costs in the world? Circle your answer: WE ARE ALL RICH AND CAN AFFORD IT...THE DRUG COMPANIES JACK UP THE PRICES TO MAKE MORE MONEY...WE LET OUR LEGISLATORS CONTROL OUR

LIVES INSTEAD OF THEM WORKING FOR US.

The United States is the only country in the free world that does not have universal health coverage. Does this mean the Unites States is smarter than the rest of the world or behind the times? Circle your answer: SMARTER...BEHIND THE TIMES...

"I have always wondered why teeth are not included in normal health insurance policies." Vent said. "Teeth as far as I am concerned are an important part of our body."

Why is it teeth are never considered in health insurance legislation when they are a part of your body? Circle your answer: I REALLY DON'T KNOW...THEY ARE NOT A PART OF A PERSON'S BODY...THE GOVERNEMENT IS STUPID...PEOPLE DON'T CARE IF THEY HAVE TEETH...

There are separate insurance policies for your teeth but unless you are purchasing them through your employer they are cost prohibitive.

What is your solution to the health care problem in the United States? Your idea:

____

____

"The President just announced he will not allow transgender people to join the military," I said.

"If I was transgender it wouldn't bother me if I couldn't join the military," Vent said. "Why would anyone who has been the brunt of prejudice from the majority of people and the government even want to serve their country?"

If you were transgender would you want to serve the country? Circle YES or NO and your reasoning:

____

____

For that matter if you were a minority that has been the brunt of unfair laws and prejudice would you have any desire to serve your country? Circle YES or NO...a space for your reasoning:

____

____

“99.5% of Americans do not join the military,” Vent said.

“With our low enlistment rate we sure have a lot of people who are always ranting how they want a strong military,” I said.

“Most of them are armchair generals that when they were old enough to join the military they backed out with one excuse or another,” Vent said. “Now they like to scream and shout how the country is becoming weak when in all truth they are the reason the country is becoming weak. I hate to say it but in my opinion people who want a strong military, but have not served, do not have the right to open their mouths.”

“If I had my way every young man and woman when they reached 18 years old would have to enlist for two years in one of the military branches. This means rich kids, poor kids, white kids, Mexican kids, all races of kids, kids with flat feet could work in an office, if you had one arm or one leg there is something you could do, no excuses, no exceptions," I said.

"There could also be a law if you have not served your country you cannot vote or be elected in any political post either federal or state level," Vent added.

"It would solve the health insurance issue," I said. "Everyone would be enrolled in the VA after they got out."

"The government would then try and privatize the VA and make it a zillion dollar enterprise. At which time they would lower the taxes on the rich and make the middle class pick up the slack," Vent said.

What do you think about everyone man and women at age 18, with no exceptions, having to serve at least two years in the military? Those who object to fighting under religious reasons would be given a non-combat job or jobs that benefit society. Circle your answer YES or NO...and your reasoning:

____

____

Those who refused to be inducted would be shipped to the country of their choice and have their citizenship taken away. Is that fair? Circle your answer YES or NO...

Those who refused to serve might find it difficult to find a country that would want them.

Do you think you should have to serve your country to earn the right to vote? Circle YES or NO...a space for your reasoning:

"There are 82 veterans in the House of Representatives, two of which are women?" Vent said.

How many people are in the House of Representatives? Circle your answer:

100...125...175...200...250...300...350...400...435...450...500.

There are 435 members in the House of Representatives?

"20 members of the Senate are veterans," Vent added.

How many people are members of the Senate? Circle your answer: 50...75...100...

The answer is 100.

Out of 535 people who run our country 102 are veterans.

President Trump's avoided the draft four times for being in college and one time for bad feet. I take it by all the rounds of golf he plays his feet are fully recovered.

Do you think President Trump's feet were ever hurt enough to avoid the draft? Circle YES or NO...

Do you think the people in the House of Representatives and the Congress who served in the military respect our draft dodging president? Circle YES or NO...

Do you think people who did not serve in the military should be able to run for public office when in all truth they have made no sacrifices for this country? Circle YES or NO...a space for your reasoning: I must admit I am prejudiced because I am a veteran.

____

If you circled YES that people who did not serve in the military should not be able to hold public office would you please start a campaign to get rid of all the cowards we have elected to public office.

If you circled NO do you think being a politician is a hard job and a great sacrifice for your country? Circle YES or NO...

If you think being a politician is hard job and a great sacrifice here is a space for you to explain why.

____

____

If you do not think being a politician is a hard job here is a space for you to list a few hard jobs: I will state a few: Miner, construction worker, good cop, cowboy...

____

____

"What do you think about the controversy over Southern Civil War Statues and the Confederate Flag?" I asked Vent.

"The confederate flag is no different than the Nazi flag. It is a flag of suppression and hate.

Statues glorifying the confederacy are ludicrous. What most people don't know is the statues to honor confederate heroes were not raised immediately after the war but were erected by the Daughters of the Confederacy after the war when the main Southern objective was to block the black vote and strengthen Jim Crow laws," Vent said. "But I do not think the statues or flags should be destroyed. They could be placed in museums with information that tells the truth concerning the history behind them."

Isn't it about time both Yankees and Southerners got over the Civil War? Circle YES or NO...

Why is the south so obsessed with the Civil War when they got their asses kicked? Your answer:

___

___

Is freedom of speech at times given too much leeway? YES or NO...

"There are several states in the south where high school history books state black people were imported from Africa to WORK on plantations – there is no mention of slavery," Vent said.

Should schools be required to teach the truth? Circle YES or NO...

Did the slaves sing songs and dance as they were boarding slave ships looking forward to a great life of picking cotton, being beaten, and living in poverty? Circle your answer YES or NO...

"I have a trivia question for you," Vent said. "At the time of the Civil War what was the percentage of poor whites to rich whites in the south?

"I have no idea," I answered. "Truthfully I have never thought about it."

Do you have any idea? Circle your answer: THERE WERE NO POOR WHITE

PEOPLE IN THE SOUTH...33%...50%...60%...75%...

2/3rds of all white people in the south were subsistence farmers who barely skimped by and did not have enough money to own slaves. There were approximately

1,500 extremely wealthy families who owned the majority of the land and at the same time delegated almost 100% of the power. The main reason that poor southerner's condoned slavery was the fact they could feel superior to someone. Do you find this interesting or not. Circle your answer INTERESTING... NOT INTERESTING...

Did you know that during the Civil War a man drafted into the Northern Army could pay another person to take his place? Circle YES or NO...

The answer is YES.

Because of this there were few wealthy people who fought in the war and lead to the statement: "The Civil War was a rich man's war fought by the poor."

Did you know that at the beginning of the war Lincoln stopped black soldiers from joining the Northern Army which boosted the southern cause that white men were better than black men. Circle YES or NO...

Did you know that in text books in Oklahoma there is no mention of the slaughter of Native Americans? Circle YES or NO...

Is it morally right for history to be altered? Circle YES or NO...

In our modern times, and so called free country, here are the top ten banned books in America for this year: THE CATCHER IN THE RYE by J.D. Salinger, THE GREAT GATSBY by F. Scott Fitzgerald, TO KILL A MOCKINGBIRD by Harper Lee, LORD OF THE FLIES by William

Golding, 1984 by George Orwell, THE GRAPES OF WRATH by John Steinbeck, THE COLOR PURPLE by Alice Walker, ULYSSES by James Joyce, LOOKING FOR ALASKA by John Green, BELOVED by Toni Morrison, LOLITA by Vladimir Nabokov.

People and governments can ask for books to be banned because of language, sex, religion, opinion. There are currently over 100 banned books in the United States. The majority of banned books are in the southern states.

Should any state, person, or agency be able to tell you what you can and cannot read? Circle YES or NO...

Should a state, person, or agency be able to lie about their history? Circle YES or NO...

Is there any country in the world that's history is not filled with propaganda and lies? Circle YES or NO...

If you answered YES list the countries:

____

____

If you listed the United States you had better dig deeper into the history books, not the ones taught in high school.

Does the past in anyway affect your life? Circle YES or NO...

Do thoughts of the future in anyway affect your life? Circle YES or NO...

If your answer to the two above questions was NO here is a space to write what does affect your life:

"If ISIS and Al-Qaeda are labeled terrorist groups do you think the KKK and White Supremist should also be labeled terrorist groups?" Vent asked. Circle your answer YES or NO...and your reasoning either way:

If the KKK and White Supremist groups were labeled terrorist groups should their members be hunted down and incarcerated at Guantanamo Bay Prison in Cuba without a trial or a specific charge? Circle YES or NO...

If the KKK and White Supremist groups are not terrorist groups what are they? Your answer:

Is placing a cross in a person's yard and lighting it on fire a terrorist act? Circle YES or NO...

Is preaching that Jews and any race that is not white should be exterminated a terrorist act? Circle your answer YES or NO...

If there was a black or Hispanic organization that marched with robes and hoods on and called for the extermination of white people do you think they would be labeled a terrorist organization? Circle your answer YES or NO...

If there was an African American militia that went to major protests dressed in camouflaged army uniforms, wearing bullet proof vests and ammo pouches over-flowing with bullets, and clutching M-16s in their hands do you think the police would treat them differently than they do the white militia units that attend White Supremist and KKK rallies. Circle YES or NO...

"Do you think violent protest against the KKK and other hate groups does any good," I asked Vent.

"I think hate groups are realizing they might get killed spewing their prejudiced ideas and some of them are having second thoughts," Vent said. "For years no one stood up to them. On the other hand the counter protesters might gain more public support by protesting non-violently."

Do you think people participating in KKK and White Supremist rallies should be attacked and beaten up? Circle YES or NO...your reasoning:

____

____

Recently groups that attacked KKK and White Supremist rallies have come under verbal attack by people who say they are infringing on the right to free speech. Do you think this is correct? Circle YES or NO...and a space for your reasoning:

Isn't beating the hell out of a Nazi expressing your right to free speech? Circle YES or NO...

"The government should round up all the skin heads, Nazis, and all the other hate groups and militias, and drop them in the middle of nowhere with enough supplies to build a shelter, three months worth of food, all the guns they want, and tell them if they try to leave they will be tossed in jail for a minimum of 50 years," I said.

"It would work," Vent said, "but for some reason society lets the haters go on with their spiteful ways."

According to the Southern Poverty Law center there are over 800 hate groups in the United States that are divided between members of the KKK, Anti Muslim, General Hate, White Nationalist, Neo-Nazi, Skin Heads, Anti-LGBT, Neo-Confederate, Christian Identity, and Black Separatist. So far during the Trump administration hate groups have witnessed a 30% rise in activity and the F.B.I. worries more about American terrorism than attacks by foreign hate groups.

Why does society let the hate groups exist? Your answer:

At the moment the white race is close to 68% of the total population of the United States with the Hispanics and Latinos having the largest share after that. Interestingly Asian immigrants are the largest accepted immigrant society. And one-half of the children under five in the United States are minorities. According to the United States Census by 2043 the white race will be a minority in the United States.

Do you think it is time to have your children learn Spanish or Chinese? Circle YES or NO...

Or should the whole world have to learn English? Circle YES or NO...

"Do you think young people are less prejudiced than older people?" I asked Vent and will ask you: Circle YES or NO...and a space for your reasoning:

____

____

"As of 2017 high school and college students were 27% less prejudice than 10 years ago," Vent said. "The study suggests that access to the internet and mass communication educates young people far beyond the scope of their immediate environment or the prejudices of their parents and peers. Although it is proven as people grow older they also grow more prejudice."

For those of you reading this who are over 40 have you noticed your ideas about life and people have changed in a negative way? Circle YES or NO...

Or as you have aged have you grown more benevolent? Circle YES or NO...

"I have grown more trusting of people," I said.

"You are apprehensive about love," Vent said.

"I cannot deny it," I said.

"I told you when you were in Kansas City my wife died," Vent said. "After she died I had no desire to be in love again. Instead I put all my effort into becoming what I am, an orator of what I feel is wrong with society."

"Do you ever wish at times you would have fallen in love again?" I asked.

"I have pondered the question more than once, but, there is no answer to the question as I never fell in love again," Vent said.

How many times have you fallen in love? Circle your answer: ONCE...TWICE... THREE TIMES...FOUR TIMES...TOO MANY TIMES...NOT ENOUGH TIMES...NEVER...

Is love the most important aspect of being alive? Circle YES or NO...and your reasoning:

____

____

"Would you like another cup of coffee?" I asked.

"No, I have changed my mind I would enjoy another martini. If I drink too much all I have to do is walk to my room," Vent replied with a contented smile.

We ordered a gin and tonic and a martini. "Will you be able to drive?" Vent asked.

I counted the amount of alcohol we had consumed during the day and it was slightly excessive. "If I shouldn't drive I will call a cab. The ramifications of a DUI are way beyond my means," I said.

In most states a first offense DUI will cost around $5,000 and the guilty one will have an alcohol monitor installed on their vehicle and do many hours of public service.

Do you think the penalty should be stronger? Circle YES or NO...

In Texas three DUI convictions can lead to a life sentence in prison. Is this too strong of a punishment? Circle YES or NO...

If one of your loved ones was killed by a drunk driver what do you think the penalty should be? Your answer:

____

____

We did not talk until the drinks were delivered.

"I should tell you something," Vent said in a tone it made me apprehensive. "I have not been truthful concerning my visit to Phoenix. I did not come to see an old friend but for an appointment at the Mayo Hospital to get another opinion on my condition."

I felt like all the air had been sucked out of my lungs and after a few moments managed to say, "But you answered my letter months ago. Shouldn't you have come sooner?"

"I have a rare cancer. There is no need to go into a prolonged and deep explanation but I have been to several doctors in Kansas City and one in St. Louis. The doctor in St. Louis called the Mayo Hospital here in Phoenix and set up an appointment for me. He said it was worth a try."

"So that is where you were today," I said.

He nodded and sipped his martini. "I get the final diagnosis tomorrow. Then I will decide to take treatments or not," Vent said with no hint of fear or distress in his voice.

What would you say to a person who may be dying? You must fight? Circle YES or NO...

Do you say there is always hope? Circle YES or NO...

Do you say it is God's will? Circle YES or NO...

Do you say you are fucked? Circle YES or NO...

Do you say why don't you add me to your will? Circle YES or NO....

Here is room for you to write what you would say:

____

____

"Julia told me she thought you were ill," I said.

"A retired nurse would know. I will say it has been quite the experience. Poked and prodded, x-rayed and scanned, so many blood tests I thought I might run out of blood. And through it all the nurses and doctors are always doing their best to be upbeat, but underneath the smiles and good wishes you can see they know the truth. Some people beat cancer and some do not."

"You do not seem to be terrible afraid," I said.

"Even as a young boy I accepted death," Vent said. "I have always understood death is always one millionth of a second away. Death itself is not cruel or vengeful. It is only death. A part of life one has to accept and come to grips with."

Have you come to grips with death? Circle YES or NO...space for your thoughts:

____

____

"There was an article I read that stated in time science will defeat death," I said.

“For that to be true several problems have to be solved,” Vent said. “Accidental death must be eliminated, all disease must be cured, man must figure out how to feed an unlimited amount of people, and not have wars.”

Do you think there is anyway to defeat accidental death? Circle YES or NO...

Do you think science will defeat all disease? Circle YES or NO...

Do you believe man will find a way to stop having wars? Circle YES or NO...

Do you think scientists will figure out a way to feed all the people on earth? Circle YES or NO...

If mankind really cared about feeding all the starving people should they stop pouring milk down the drain to maintain a higher market value? Circle YES or NO...

Should they stop limiting crop production to maintain a higher market? Circle YES or NO...

Why doesn’t the government give all surplus food to food banks? Circle your answer: THEY DIDN’T THINK ABOUT IT...IT WOULD BE TOO MUCH WORK...THE POOR DO NOT CONTRIBUTE TO THE G.N.P...IT WOULD COST TOO MUCH...

Why is it that when anything humanitarian needs to be done the first thing politicians talk about is the prohibitive cost but when the military requests a billion dollar plane or ship it is no big deal? Your answer:

____

____

“Do you think about your death?” Vent asked.

"Getting killed scared me when I was in Vietnam but since then I have always accepted my death. I have a will for my few meager possessions and a paid burial plan with instructions as to where I want my ashes scattered," I said.

"People always say to do what you want during your life because you will grow old and regret many things," Vent said. "My problem with that is, you can only do what you want if you have money."

Can you follow your heart and do what you want to do with your life if you do not have money? Circle YES or NO...

If you answered YES please explain how you can do what you want during your life with no money. Becoming a monk is not an answer but becoming an artist or writer is:

____

____

What is the percentage of people in the United States who have been able to do what they truly wanted to do during their lifetime? 5%...10%...20%...30%...40%...50%...60%...there is no need to list 100% because it is impossible.

Only 6% of people ever realize their dreams.

Is this the reason fantasy novels are so popular? Circle YES or NO...

Could it also be a reason the crime rate in the United States is one of the highest in the world? Circle YES or NO...

"Life gives each individual their own path," Vent said. "Some life paths are sad, some life paths are filled with grief, some life paths last only a few days, some have long lives. There is no rhyme or reason to life. No matter what the doctor's say tomorrow I have been fortunate in life. I have never been hungry. I have always had a place to live and up until a few months ago my health was good."

Circle the things that you feel are important in life: MONEY...JEWELRY...FANCY CARS…OWNING A BIG HOUSE…HEALTH…LOVE…CHARITY…PRIDE…A GOLD WATCH…A LOVING SPOUSE…A PRIVATE JET…list things you think are important.

____

____

Vent finished his martini. "I should be back here by late afternoon tomorrow," he said. "It would be nice to get together one more time. I leave early the following morning."

"I would be happy to take you to the hospital," I said.

"I would rather do this by myself but thank you for the offer."

"Call me when you get back and I will come over," I said, adding, "But no ifs, ands, or buts, I will take you to the airport."

"There is no need for you to go out of your way," Vent said.

"I insist," I said.

I watched Vent until he was out of the bar and then slowly finished my gin and tonic. The noise from the bar did not invade my mind. The bill paid and with a heavy heart I headed for the sanctuary of my apartment. I do not fear death but it makes me sad when my friends are dying.

Back home I did not phone Julia but fell wearily on the sofa and thought about several happenings in my life that were life changing.

Are there times in your life when you recollect portions of your life and they are so vivid it is like you are living the memory once again? Circle YES or NO...

I do not remember falling asleep on the sofa. I was in a land of no thoughts, no dreams, and no feelings.

Julia phoned while I was frying a healthy breakfast of bacon and eggs with toast drenched in real butter. Would you give up fried bacon for an additional year or two of being alive? Circle YES or NO...

Do you think real butter is bad for you? Circle YES or NO...

Do you think most food we enjoy is bad for you? Circle YES or NO...

Are you concerned about what you eat? Circle YES or NO...

Would you stand in the middle of a strawberry field while a crop duster was spraying pesticides? Circle YES or NO...

If you answered YES here is room to explain why you are not stupid:

____

____

I could get into all the benefits I receive from the VA from being exposed to Agent Orange but there is no need.

After a few minutes of small talk with Julia I informed her about Vent. "It is too bad you have been friends for only a short time," she commented.

During the day I straightened my closet, shined several pairs of shoes I seldom wear, and did many other time consuming things one does to take their mind off of things that are bothering them. Here is a space for you to write down a few things you do to pass the time when you are nervous or bothered:

____

____

The phone rang at 3 in the afternoon. Answering I could hear my heart pounding in my ears. "I think it is time for a late afternoon martini. Meet me in the hotel bar," Vent said in a normal tone.

"I'll be there as fast as I can," was all I managed to reply.

Phoenix in the winter is the get away location for those fortunate enough to leave behind the numbing ice and snow of the Midwest and Canada. Most Midwestern people and Canadians do not understand that when the speed limit sign states 65 mph in Phoenix it really means 85 mph. More people are killed going too slow than too fast. Every lane I sped into I got behind someone doing 65 mph.

In April and May the people from the Midwest and Canadians scurry back to the land of trees and green grass. They discuss with their neighbors the difference between dry heat and humid heat and they can't understand why there are so many Hispanics in Arizona. When I visit the Midwest or Canada I wonder where all the white people come from.

Having lived in both the Midwest and Phoenix I can attest that 95 degrees in the summer in Iowa when the humidity is 92% is ten times more miserable than 100 degrees in Phoenix. I should add it is not as miserable as walking through a jungle with a radio on your back when it is 105 degrees and the humidity is never below 92% - this is true even when you are not getting shot at. I guess those unfortunate enough to be serving in Afghanistan can at least say the humidity is low even though the war is stupid. Question? Does the humidity being low in Afghanistan make the war less stupid? Circle your answer YES or NO...

Question? Can you truthfully tell a soldier returning from Afghanistan that what he experienced has anything to do with your freedom? Circle your answer YES or NO...your reasoning:

____

____

When I arrived Vent was half way through his martini and had ordered me a gin and tonic. "It is a good day when you can be in a comfortable bar and sip on a martini," Vent said.

"Have you ever thought what your life would have been like if you didn't drink?"

I asked.

"I would be richer," Vent replied. "But, think of the money that would have been kept out of circulation, and the tips bartenders and waitresses would have missed. It would have been an enormous drain on our economy."

For those of you who drink alcohol have you ever thought how much your drinking has enriched the economy? Circle YES or NO...

"What did the doctors tell you?" I asked, unable to hide my concern.

Vent sipped his martini, set the glass down, looked me straight in the eyes and said pragmatically. “William, they told me I have between three months and at the most six months to live. They said if I wanted to undergo the rigors of chemo it could extend my life maybe six or seven more months but a cure is out of the question. I told them I would not do chemo. They told me when I got back to Kansas City have my doctor write a prescription for pain pills for when the cancer progresses to the critical stage. I will tell my doctor I want pills that will not affect my mind if that is at all possible.”

“Years ago when I tried being a hippie I always wondered if I ate all at the same time a tab of acid, a tab of mescaline, shot up some heroin, smoked a gram of hash and two joints, took a tab of speed, and the combination of the drugs killed me if I would know I was dead,” I said in an attempt to hide my feelings of utter helplessness and grief.

“That’s funny,” Vent replied, “but also a good question.”

Question? If you are so stoned, drunk, messed up on anything, and you die do you know you are dead? Circle YES or NO...

If a person eats mushrooms (not the kind that people put on pizza), dreams they are one with the universe and dies do their molecules become stars? Circle YES or NO...

“I knew a lot of old hippies that swore marijuana cured everything from ingrown toenails to cancer,” Vent said. “Funny thing is most of them are dead.”

“Drugs for sure didn’t help the longevity of most rock stars,” I said.

“Marijuana does help with pain and nausea,” Vent said. “But I would rather be straight when I die.”

Do you really care if you are coherent when you die? Circle YES or NO...

I drank half of my gin and tonic. "I don't know what to say except I'm sorry," I said truthfully.

"There is nothing to say that will change anything," Vent said. "You could say 'I am sorry you are dying' and I could reply 'me too.' You could say, 'damn what shitty luck,' and I could agree. The one good thing about knowing you are going to die is it gets rid of all the guessing."

Vent waived for another round of drinks. "Didn't you mention to me you would like to buy a RV and ask Julia if she wanted to travel and see the country for a year or so?" Vent asked.

"I did, but it is more of a pipe dream than a reality. The thought is great but the reality is scary," I answered.

"If you are afraid of the cost buy the RV on time, take out a life insurance policy incase you die to pay off your debts, and hit the road."

If you had the chance, even if you might end up broke, would you buy a RV and spend a year or so traveling around the country? Circle YES or NO...

"Have you even asked Julia if she would go?" Vent asked.

"No."

"Why not?

"I really don't know," I replied.

"She has her retirement from nursing. With your two incomes there is no way you couldn't afford it," Vent said.

"What if she or I got sick?" I said.

"What if you got sick while sitting on your butt in front of the TV?" Vent asked.

Is the idea of sickness an excuse for not exploring life if you have a chance? Circle YES or NO...

Is the reason we do not take chances, even though we want to, because we are afraid to step outside of our comfort zone even if our comfort zone is boring and not where we truly want to be? Circle YES or NO...a space to explain why we should or should not step out of our comfort zone:

____

____

"What will you do now?" I asked Vent.

"I will update my will and try and find a literary agent to represent my novels."

"You never told me what your novels are about."

"They are not westerns, romances, science fiction, or any thing that can be labeled," Vent said. "My novels are about thoughts, and dreams, and probabilities, and other magical things that stretch the imagination and hopefully make people think."

"I would like to read them," I said hoping Vent would tell me he would send me a few to read but he did not reply.

If you were a writer would you let people read your unpublished novels? Circle YES or NO....and your reasoning:

____

____

"Are you in pain?" I asked deeply concerned.

"Nothing I cannot handle at the moment. I tire easily but I really don't want to sleep all the time. My time means more to me now than it ever has," Vent answered.

"There are several states that have right to die laws. If you are fatally ill they will prescribe the necessary pills to commit a painless suicide," I said.

"It is a good law but I don't think I am brave enough to take my own life," Vent said.

Do you think assisted suicide is wrong? Circle YES or NO...your reasoning:

____

____

Do you think one must be brave to commit suicide if they know they have an incurable disease and are going to die? Circle YES or NO...and your reasoning:

____

____

Could you take your own life if you knew you were dying from a disease and did not want to go through the agony? Circle YES or NO...your reasoning:

____

____

"I find it both ironic and sad that I have spent years ranting and raving about governments and police and injustice and I don't think I have been able to change a thing," Vent said. "I could have just as well walked around with a sign stating THE WORLD IS ENDING and accomplished as much."

"You have changed my opinion about a lot of things," I consoled.

"I suppose changing opinions can make the world change for the good,"

Vent said. "But, it seems as soon as one group starts doing good things for people there are other groups filled with hate and malice that overshadow them."

"I have to agree," I replied.

"Maybe the world is destined to always be overshadowed by hate and greed and prejudice and those who stand against these things are destined to always be a minority," Vent said.

Do you think hate and greed and prejudice will always overshadow those who do not hate, are not greedy, or are not prejudice? Circle your answer YES or NO...and your reasoning:

____

____

Do you think there are more good people in the world than bad? Circle YES or NO...

According to many studies it is estimated that 80% of the people in the world are good hearted with good intentions. It is the other 20% that are downright scary.

Would it be terrible if one day the 80% united and said we are going to do one terribly bad thing in our lives and completely destroyed the 20% of bad people? Circle your answer: IT

WOULD BE TERRIBLE...IT WOULD NOT BE TERRIBLE...WHAT ARE THE GOOD PEOPLE WAITING FOR...

The waitress brought the drinks. “Make sure I get the bill,” Vent said, adding, “and this is for you,” and placed a twenty dollar bill on her tray.

“Sir, that is way too much,” she said and held the bill out for Vent to take back.

“No my dear it is not enough,” Vent replied.

The waitress walked away with a bounce in her step. “Have you ever noticed hard working people and those with little always seem to be more caring?” Vent asked.

“I think it is because they have been through many things the wealthy have never experienced,” I said.

Are hard working people more apt to help someone in need? Circle your answer YES or NO...

“During your life have you ever been so broke you could not afford food?” Vent asked.

“No, but one of the saddest things I ever saw in my life were children in Vietnam scraping the inside grooves of metal garbage cans with spoons and eating the greasy residue,” I said.

“Have you ever thought that maybe we are on Earth because we have been sent here for punishment?” Vent asked.

Is Earth really hell? Circle YES or NO...your reasoning:

____

____

If you are a Catholic is there a chance Earth might be purgatory? Circle YES or

NO...

“To change the subject, did you know that Alexander Hamilton, one of our venerated founding fathers, stated that for a country to prosper the biggest labor source that should be exploited was women and children?” I stated.

“I knew that,” Vent said.

“Did you know this? Circle YES or NO...

“Did you know that the Founding Fathers really didn’t care about the poor but thought that the poverty problem would be solved if the majority of poor people migrated west in search of a better life?” I asked Vent and will ask you is the above statement TRUE or FALSE...

It is true.

“It did not work because the rich were able to buy the good land and the poor just moved into another poor existence,” Vent said.

“I have a gripe about news reporters,” I said.

“Real news or fake news?” Vent asked.

“News coverage about tragedies and catastrophes?” I replied and continued. “You see coverage on the news about a family whose house has just burnt down, or their house has been flooded and everything destroyed, or a family member has been murdered, or any other terrible accident, and a reporter immediately sticks a microphone in their face and asks some stupid question like, ‘And how do you feel now that you have lost everything?’ or “What are you going to do now?’ or “How do you feel about the person who killed your son?’ What type of questions are these?”

“Stupid questions,” Vent said. “The people should scream at the reporter, ‘You idiot how do you think I feel? Do you think I want to go dancing? Take that microphone out of my face before I shove it down your throat.'"

Do you think reporters should be allowed to interview people immediately after a tragedy or catastrophe? Circle YES or NO...

If you answered YES should there be at least a minimum amount of time before reporters are allowed to interview people? Circle YES or NO...

Vent finished his drink. "Are you sure you want to take me to the airport in the morning. I have to be there by six am."

"I will be outside waiting at five," I replied.

The thought of seeing Vent for the last time left me feeling sad and alone.

Vent signaled for the bill. I accompanied Vent to the elevator. We shook hands as the elevator doors opened and as the doors closed I waved goodbye like one waves at a small child.

Have you ever been so engaged with your thoughts you do not remember driving or walking to your destination? Circle YES or NO...

How does a person do such a thing without a conscious effort? Your answer:

____

____

Realizing I was home I went to the patio.

In the city there are only a few visible stars at night. They get gobbled up by the city lights like they are something that should not exist. Maybe we should not exist I thought, which is morbid to say the least. Do you think the statement is morbid? Circle YES or NO...

When was the last time you were able to look at the night sky and see the stars?

Circle your answer: YESTERDAY...A WEEK AGO...A MONTH AGO...I DON'T REALLY THINK ABOUT THE STARS...

I saw several faded stars and made a wish. Do you believe in wishes? Circle YES or NO...or are wishes merely childhood fantasies? Circle YES or NO...

I was by the passenger side door in front of the hotel at five in the morning.

Vent walked out at exactly five minutes after five. "Good morning sir," I said opening the door and taking his bag.

"The airport my dear man and be quick about it," Vent said. "I have places to be and things to see."

"I have a question," I said as I drove toward the airport.

"Life is a question," Vent said.

"There has recently been a company that put a chip in some of their employees for identification. What is your opinion about that?"

"There will come a day when the government has instilled so much fear in people they will gladly have chips implanted in them," Vent said. "There will be your date of birth, where you live, your medical history, your criminal record, and as you grow older more data will be added. All the authorities will have to do is swipe your chip just like they do dogs and cats now."

"It is scary," I cringed.

"Big Brother is always thinking and scheming for more power," Vent responded.

Do you think there will come a day when all people will be required to have a chip implanted in them with all their information? Circle YES or NO...

Do you think having a chip implanted in your body is an overreach by the government? Circle YES or NO...and your reasoning:

____

____

Would you voluntarily let your business or the government put a chip in you? Circle YES or NO...

If you answered YES would it make you feel safer? Circle YES or NO...and if it would make you feel safer why?

____

____

Vent and I did not talk the rest of the way to the airport. There are times when silence is the best communication.

I opened the door oblivious to the rushing people and handed Vent his bag.

Vent smiled and we hugged, patting each other on the back. “The best my friend,” he said. “I wish you and Julia a long and good life.”

“The best to you,” I managed to choke out.

Vent turned. The last I saw of him was his back. He was waving his left arm up and down like the old Vent. I knew he was talking to himself.

All Julia said that evening concerning Vent was, “I hope he found some satisfaction with his life.”

I suppose that is all we can really hope for.

As the weeks passed there were many times I wanted to write Vent but I figured if Vent wanted to communicate he would write and besides he knew my phone number. I could picture him at some Zen type gathering learning how to find his center and become one with the universe before he died. Julia said he was more than likely finding his center by drinking too many martinis. I also had occasional thoughts that he might be in terrible pain and I imagined him emaciated and connected by tubes and wires to machines that performed all his necessary bodily functions. With great effort I drove away these thoughts.

Life went back to normal. Several times a week after work I went to the Italian bar for a beer. Each time Frank the bartender would comment how he liked the little weird guy from Kansas City who minded his own business. Then one Sunday Fat Tony, Slim Jim, Johnny the Wart, Billie Bundle, Frank the Nose, Frank the bartender, and everyone else I met at the bar has their photographs on the front page of the newspaper. They, along with numerous other individuals from the East Coast, were arrested for racketeering, embezzlement, murder, and conspiracy to commit every crime you can think of. Several days later I went to the bar but it was closed. A few days latter I was visited at work by two FBI agents who placed photographs of various people on my desk and wondered how many cars I had sold to these individuals. “With all due respect officers I can’t remember but as far as I know selling cars is not a crime,” I said.

“You give us the same deal on a car you gave Fat Tony?” one of the agents asked.

“Of course,” I said.

"We'll be in to buy a car," the other agent replied as they left.

Julia and I discussed buying an RV and driving into the unknown with no particular destination in mind. We both liked the idea but seemed reluctant to really do anything about it.

We did take the big step and admit we loved each other but agreed marriage was out of the question. Besides it would only mess up our Social Security. The law can get in the way of love. But, the law can get in the way of a lot of good things.

Merely out of curiosity, do you think there are too many laws? Circle YES or NO...

If you answered YES is there anything that can be done about it? A blank for your answer:

____

____

The next thing I knew it was April and the snowbirds were streaming back to Canada and the Midwest. The local bar was having a contest who could guess the date for the first day over 100 degrees. The winner would win free ice cold beer for a week.

Do you really care how hot it gets in Phoenix in the summer? Circle YES or NO...

For that matter unless you live in Alaska do you really care how cold it gets in Alaska? Circle YES or NO...

Do people really care about things unless it involves them? Circle YES or NO...your reasoning either way:

____

In late May I received a hand written letter from Vent that was not written on his monogrammed paper but on a plain sheet of typing paper. The writing was barely legible and I could tell it had taken great determination and effort to write. It read:

Dear William:

Here are a few statements I overheard in bars, in line at the grocery store, while waiting for a bus, eating out, listening to the radio, watching TV, and other normal day to day functions. Some are profound, some are funny, and some are filled with great wisdom. I will send you more at a later date. Concerning my novels, I have signed with a well known New York Literary Agent. He informed me he found them unusual, creative, interesting, caring, slightly off center, and because the world is off center there should be a market. My attorneys have all the legal ins and outs taken care of and if the books do sell any money generated will be distributed as to my wishes. As you can tell I am still alive. Cancer has taught me one thing – this dying is hard work. Take care.

Always your friend,

Samuel R. Ruthorford Jr. (Vent)

P.S. If you have not purchased an RV you are an idiot and will regret it. Hello to Julia.

HERE ARE VENT'S OVERHEAD STATEMENTS.

1) For my enemies. I am going to feed you and make you live to death.

2) What if in life there was no identification required?

3) Some is better than none.

4) They look to the stars but forget their feet are on the ground.

5) Decaf-espresso is ridiculous?

6) They say at the time of death you lose 6.2 oz of body weight. What does a soul weigh?

7) Living with her was like driving on a gravel road after one too many drinks and looking for the center line.

8) You could be the burly type if you weren't so small.

9) Sign in a bar that was never taken down – Free Beer Tomorrow.

10) The stars over a city are nothing more than an illusion.

11) Migration of the snails. (mentioned at a bus station)

12) When Ray died we each took an arm and screwed him into the ground – that's how crooked he was.

13) Silence has no answers.

14) If you have to rush to get somewhere there is a problem.

15) People are easy to frighten especially by politicians.

16) A man or woman's only true friend is a dog.

17) Trust your enemies, you know they are lying.

18) If alcohol was good for you it would contain vitamins and fiber.

19) Would you want your bus driver or cab driver or airline pilot to be high on marijuana?

20) Modern life is not based on good or bad – it is based on expense and revenue.

21) Why do automobiles depreciate 20% as soon as they are driven off the lot?

22) The way to get an honest politician. If the first one messes up hang him. If the next one messes up hang him. The third one will do a good job.

23) The only problem with me writing a book is the words.

24) I could lose weight if I wasn't hungry all the time.

25) A country is not a democracy if the popular vote does not count.

26) Send me all your poor and those ravaged by war except Muslims and Mexicans.

27) Somehow Christians have forgotten what Christianity is.

28) There can't be anything wrong with the pesticides I spray on my crops. It kills everything it comes in contact with.

29) Every person who does not believe in a woman's right to have an abortion should have to adopt three children.

30) Most people believe in the military as long as they don't have to serve.

31) Rich men start wars – poor men fight them.

32) Alternative power sources are the wave of the future. That is why the government wants to cut their funding.

33) It is easy to slam welfare until you are laid off and your unemployment runs out.

34) I bought a semi-automatic rifle with a 50 round clip just incase the squirrels try and invade the country.

35) The way the economy is going downhill I will have to sell one of my three cars.

36) I'd eat more fish if hamburger wasn't so cheap.

37) The only way out of here is the wrong way.

38) Life is not wasted only on the young – the majority of life is wasted.

39) When I was a kid I worked for a dollar an hour and I was poor. After high school I worked for three dollars an hour and I was poor. Later in life I worked for ten dollars an hour and I was still poor. When wages hit fifteen dollars an hour I will still be poor. Rich people have a way of figuring it out.

40) Killed on a one way street looking the wrong way.

41) If you believe the south fought the Civil War for states rights you are a victim of propaganda or stupid.

42) When the Supreme Court ruled corporations are people then what exactly are human beings? When I look in a mirror I don't see a corporation.

43) The dumbing down of America is real. Look at what books are popular.

44) Why is it when something tastes or smells terrible people always want someone else to taste or smell it?

45) One regret I have in my life is, I should have gone fishing more.

46) One should dance even if they are a terrible dancer.

47) Trying to become a member of the crowd is degrading.

48) Individual thought does not nurture in a herd.

49) The search for true history is the task of a scholar.

50) Starving people do not concern themselves with the food pyramid.

When I finished reading I could envision Vent in my mind's eye frantically jotting down each statement.

That evening Julia read the letter. "He had a wonderful mind," she said.

"I see him as a cross between Will Rogers and Mark Twain but with a streak of anger," I said.

"Humor is anger," she said.

As each day rolled into another there was not a time I did not think about Vent. The thoughts were not sad but they were also not happy. I cannot define them. The one thing that really bothered me was the idea I probably would not be notified when he died.

Have you ever lost touch with a friend and wondered if they have died? Circle your answer YES or NO...

Do you think a dead person knows how many people are attending their funeral?

Circle YES or NO...

Do you really care how many people attend your funeral? Circle YES or NO...

Do you think that in many ways the modern funeral is morbid? Circle YES or NO...

Why is the deceased at funerals always loving, good hearted, great with kids, and will be a loss to the community? Your answer:

____

____

If there are so many good people dying then we should never have wars or any kind of strife. I read an article in the newspaper where three members of an outlaw Texas motorcycle gang had been gunned down by a member of a rival gang. According to the obituary all three of the deceased were upright, loveable, a bonus to the community, and great family members. Do you think outlaw motorcycle gangs are a great asset to society? Circle YES or NO...

One of the mourning gang members made a statement to the press, and I quote, "Our brother is now driving his Harley in heaven."

"Do you think there are Harleys in heaven? Circle YES or NO...

It was a normal June day, the radio announcer informed the public the low temperature would be 92 degrees and the high would be 109 degrees. Warnings had been issued not to leave children or pets in cars and stay hydrated.

Do you think people who leave children or pets in hot cars should go to jail? Circle YES or NO...your reasons why?

____

____

For those of you who have children have you ever forgotten your child in a grocery store or at a friends? Circle YES or NO...if you have should you be in jail? Circle YES or NO....or was it an honest mistake brought on by the daily frustrations of life? Circle YES or NO...

I know men and women who wished they had forgotten their first wives or husbands but that is a different matter all together.

The warning to stay hydrated I thought was stupid. Do you know anyone who does not drink water when it is 100 degrees? Circle YES or NO...

I was at work and not busy because sane people do not venture out in the middle of the afternoon to shop for cars during the summer in Phoenix. A man, who I estimated was in his mid-forties, dressed in an expensive summer suit and carrying a brown leather briefcase approached my desk. “You must work for the government to have to wear a suit during the summer,” I said.

“No, I work for a very prestigious law firm that believes those who do not wear a suit and tie are heathens,” he said with a friendly smile.

“If someone is trying to sue me I don’t own a house or have a great deal of money,” I said.

“Did you know that in New Zealand it is extremely hard to sue?” he asked.

I shook my head wondering if I could talk Julia into moving to New Zealand, denounce our American citizenship, and becoming New Zealanders. In America suing is the way to riches – ask our president or ask the 4,000 people that are suing him.

Has the ability to sue gotten out of hand in the United States? Circle YES or NO...

“Are you William Brown?” the lawyer asked.

“Are you here to buy a car?” I asked not confirming my name. I am cautious when people ask me who I am without any clarification as to why. I learned this from Jimmy the Nose.

“I live in Manhattan and do not own a car,” he replied. “Nor do I wish to own one.”

“I don’t blame you one bit,” I said.

“I am James Medafore. I work for the law firm of Branchett, Levit, and Kaufman. We specialize in large estate management.”

“I gather Samuel R. Ruthorford Jr. has died,” I said, relieved his suffering was over but also deeply saddened he was gone.

“I am William Brown,” I said wondering why Mr. Medafore wanted to see me.

“I need to see a form of identification,” Mr. Medafore said.

I showed him my driver’s license and VA card.

Mr. Medafore opened his briefcase. “Mr. Ruthorford wanted these delivered to you personally. Neither I nor anyone at the firm knows what is in the envelopes,” he said handing me a sealed personal sized envelope with my name written on the front and a business sized manila envelope, also sealed, with my name written on the front.

“If you would sign this paper confirming you have received the two envelopes I will be happy to leave this hell hole and return to the congested streets of Manhattan,” he said handing me a paper to sign along with a gold pen.

I signed the paper.

“Mr. Ruthorford was cremated and his ashes were buried next to his wife. His vast fortune is in the process of being distributed as to his wishes. Although he was eccentric he was a kind hearted and good man,” Mr. Medafore said. “I had the privilege of working with him for many years. He also wanted me to deal with his literary agent, which I am happy to do, and I can assure you everything will be done in a professional and honorable way.”

“He was a dear friend of mine,” I said.

Before Mr. Medafore departed he gave me his card to contact him if there were any questions concerning the contents of the two envelopes or to get information on Vent’s novels.

I gazed at the two envelopes on my desk. Part of me wanted to rip them open immediately. Another part of me wanted to put them in the back of a drawer and forget they existed. I did not touch them and spent the rest of the afternoon thinking about Vent.

At home that evening I put the envelopes on the kitchen table and got a beer. I raised my beer in a toast to the envelopes, “To you Vent, it was my pleasure to know you.”

In the small envelope was a check made out to me for $150,000. There was nothing else. I looked at the check and really did not know what to think. I was flabbergasted to say the least. If out of the blue someone gave you a check for $150,000 would you be in shock? Circle YES or NO...

Would it be a life changer? Circle YES or NO...

Would you care if you had to pay taxes on it? Circle YES or NO...

Would you wish it had been cash so you would not have to claim it? Circle YES or NO...

Would you immediately do something stupid like fly to Vegas and lose it all? Circle YES or NO...

Would you run out and waste it on a new car, gold watch, or other materialistic stuff that in a few weeks would lose its luster? Circle YES or NO...

I finished the beer and got another one. Isn't it strange the many reasons people drink alcohol? Here is a place for you to list the many reasons people drink alcohol. I will state a few: People drink because they are happy, sad, and:

____

____

Inside the manila envelope was a brochure for a new Class C motor home. It was the top of the line and came with every bell and whistle imaginable. Paper-clipped to the last page of the brochure was the title and registration for the motor home in Julia's and my name, an insurance policy for full coverage paid for one year which included road side assistance, an extended warranty (which I think are rip-offs), membership to a network of motor home camping sites around the country that came with a 15% discount, and a list of companies that worked on motor homes. There was also a typed letter.

Dear William:

Enjoy – whenever possible give a helping hand.

It was not signed.

I went through all the material again hoping Vent had enclosed more of his overheard statements but there were not any.

ONE YEAR LATER: 25 MILES NORTH OF VANCOUVER, BRITISH COLOMBIA

Julia and I sold everything we owned that would not fit in the camper and what did not sell we gave to various organizations that assist those in need. I donated one half of the money Vent gave me to various charities and Julia and I have in our wills her children will get what remains. Over the last year, with no set direction in mind, Julia and I have camped in every continental state except Alaska, which we are now headed for. After Alaska we will decide on our next destination. It has been a peaceful year, more a year of finding ourselves and each other, and also meeting many fine people from around the country. We do not follow the news and the world has managed to go on without our help. The camper came equipped with two TV's but we had them removed. If we wish to watch a special show we go to a bar. We occasionally go to a movie but normally in the evening we sit outside. We also play games and read. We nick named the camper VENT which I had painted in the center of the bumper. When people ask about the name I tell them he was a dear friend of mine. I had copies made of Vent's overheard statements and if people want to know more about him I give them a copy. I do wonder what happened to the other bits of overheard statements Vent was going to send me. It is a great loss they will never be shared. Julia believes one day someone will be at a second hand store or flea market and going through an old box or desk drawer and come across them. I sincerely hope so.

Several months ago I phoned Vent's lawyer, Vent's Mr. Medafore. A prestigious literary press signed a contract for all of Vent's novels and will publish the first one next year. It is titled REFLECTIONS OF THE SUNSET. If all goes well they will publish the rest of the books at yearly intervals, which I have no doubt they will. I am anxious to read them.

I have learned life is what you make of it and feel fortunate.

Do you believe that life should have many beginnings and adventures? Circle YES or NO...

Do you think 100 years from now anyone will care what we did with our lives? Circle YES or NO...

There was one overheard statement Vent mailed me that I did not mention earlier: LIFE WOULD BE SO MUCH EASIER IF ALL RACES AND ALL RELIGIONS AND ALL BELIEFS WOULD SIMPLY BE KIND.

THE END

If you enjoyed this book would you please leave a review on your favorite book site and tell ten million people to purchase a copy so my wife and I can buy a motor home. If you would like to contact me you may leave a comment on my website: swisherbooks.com...e-mail me: swisherwritesfiction@gmail.com...or message me on Facebook.

www.ingramcontent.com/pod-product-compliance
Lightning Source LLC
Chambersburg PA
CBHW082101090726
47910CB00008B/2556

* 9 7 8 0 9 9 7 9 0 9 6 2 3 *